D0592215

MONSTER SLAYERS

MONSTER SLAYERS

Lukas Ritter

BOOKS FOR
YOUNG READERS

Monster Slayers

©2010 Wizards of the Coast LLC

Published by Wizards of the Coast LLC

DUNGEONS & DRAGONS, WIZARDS OF THE COAST, and their respective logos are trademarks of Wizards of the Coast LLC in the U.S.A. and other countries.

Printed in the U.S.A.

Cover art by Jesper Ejsing
First Printing: May 2010

9 8 7 6 5 4 3 2 1

ISBN: 978-0-7869-5484-1
620-25358000-001-EN

Library of Congress Cataloging-in-Publication Data

Ritter, Lukas, 1982-
  Monster slayers / Lukas Ritter.
    p. cm.
  Summary: On the trail of their families and other villagers who have been kidnapped by dog-like creatures, Evin and Jorick join forces with the beautiful elf Betilivatis, an apprentice wizard who is an expert on monsters.
  ISBN 978-0-7869-5484-1
  [1. Fantasy. 2. Monsters--Fiction. 3. Wizards--Fiction. 4. Witches--Fiction.] I. Title.
  PZ7.R5149Mon 2010
  [Fic]--dc22

                                                          2009045546

U.S., CANADA,
ASIA, PACIFIC, & LATIN AMERICA
Wizards of the Coast LLC
P.O. Box 707
Renton, WA 98057-0707
+1-800-324-6496

EUROPEAN HEADQUARTERS
Hasbro UK Ltd
Caswell Way
Newport, Gwent NP9 0YH
GREAT BRITAIN
Please keep this address for your records.

Visit our Web site at www.wizards.com

WC-FF   10 11 12 13 14 15 16

For Jeff Sampson, without whom this book
never would have come to be.

Chapter One

Evin blinked once, then squinted. The afternoon sun glared bright white. He raised a hand and shielded his eyes.

Tree bark bit through his trousers. Keeping his eyes shielded, he looked down between his dangling feet. Yellow grass and gnarled roots burst from the ground beneath him—far, far beneath him.

A wave of dizziness hit him. He struggled to remember exactly why he had decided to climb up into the tree.

Twigs crunched. Evin looked down again to see a boy creeping around the tree's trunk, gripping a wooden sword.

The boy's name flashed in Evin's mind.

Jorick.

Then it all came flooding back. Of course. He was playing a game—a game of ambush—with his friend Jorick. The two boys did it all the time. But this time was different. This time he had to win.

Grinning, Evin adjusted himself as quietly as he could. He reached to his side and found a carved wooden dagger attached to his belt. He waited and watched as Jorick looked left and right behind the tree trunks. Jorick didn't think to look up—he never did.

Jorick took a step forward, then another. One more step and he was positioned right where Evin wanted him.

"Aaaaaargh!" Evin screamed a war cry so loud that Jorick leaped straight up. Evin landed on Jorick's back and they tumbled into the yellow grass.

Evin twisted Jorick's arm and swung his leg around his friend's waist, pinning him down. Jorick lay facedown in the dirt.

"Cheater." Jorick lifted his head and spit. He squirmed against Evin's tight grip. "You have to give me another chance."

"No," Evin said. "I won fair and square, so tonight we're going on our adventure. Got it?"

Jorick stopped worming around. His back rose and fell rapidly, lifting Evin up and down and up and down. Though Evin couldn't see his friend's face, he knew it was twisted into a scowl.

"All right," Jorick grunted. "I give up. I'll go."

Evin loosened his grip and started to stand. "Good. I don't know why you even argued against it the first place. It's all we ever talk about."

And it was.

For as long as Evin could remember, he dreamed of leaving his village of Hesiod to travel the countryside, have grand adventures, and become a real hero like the ones he read about.

Yesterday, Evin decided he wasn't going to dream about it anymore. He was going to leave, leave for real.

It all started after Evin had finished sweeping the pub at the inn. Evin's father ran Hesiod's only inn and he expected Evin and his brother Marten to learn the trade—but all that meant was that Evin and Marten got stuck doing all the work that Father didn't want to do.

Late that afternoon, Father had found Evin and Marten practicing pick pocketing on the inn's patrons. They weren't stealing anything valuable—just handkerchiefs, like usual—but it didn't matter. Father yelled and sent Evin to his room where he'd stewed, feeling trapped behind the walls of that stupid inn.

So Evin made a plan. After Father let Marten off work for the day, he and Jorick and his brother would all set out on the adventure they'd always dreamed of, with no fathers and no ridiculous expectations.

Only, Jorick had refused to go. He had never before said no to anything Evin asked. The only way to settle it, Evin decided, was a fight into submission.

Jorick shrugged his broad shoulders as he stood.

He looked up at Evin. "Does it really have to be tonight? Can't we at least have a day to pack?"

Evin shook his head. "Nope. It has to be tonight. I'm not going to sleep in that stupid inn ever again."

"What about saying good-bye to my dad?"

"You can write him a letter, but after we're far enough away that no one can follow."

Jorick hunched down. He didn't say anything. Evin kicked him lightly in the shin.

"It will be all right, Jorick," he said. "It's not like we won't come back some day to visit and—"

Without a word, Jorick barreled toward Evin, meaty arms held wide. Evin spun to the right, ducked under Jorick's arms, spun once more, and leaped onto Jorick's exposed back. The stockier boy stumbled forward, his hands grasping at the empty space where Evin had stood only a moment before.

"You know you're never going to beat me," Evin said into Jorick's ear. "You should just stop trying."

Jorick tried to peel Evin's fingers loose. He staggered backward, deeper and deeper into the woods.

Evin laughed and hung on tight, enjoying the forced piggyback ride. Then, he felt his back hit a wall.

A sharp, electric tingle coursed through Evin's body and he yelped. His brain grew fuzzy. Goose bumps prickled his skin. Searing pain lanced the back of his shoulders, his neck, his head. Bright light reflecting off the wall seemed to envelope Evin. For a moment, his mind went blank except for two words: get away.

Evin hollered and his friend stepped forward, allowing him to fall to the dirt. Gasping for air, Evin squeezed his eyes shut to block out the light. Cool relief washed over him as the electric tingle, the fuzziness around his brain, and the heat faded away.

Squinting, Evin craned his neck to look up at the wall. It was made of ivory bricks so smoothly put together that it seemed the wall was one perfect piece of stone. The wall jutted from the ground and went all the way into the sky, so far that it became obscured behind misty clouds that floated lazily in the sky. The wall ran forever into the horizon in either direction, disappearing into a haze behind the forest's trees.

It had always been here, this wall. Well, for as long as Evin could remember anyway. He used to come and stare at it when he was younger, always wondering if it was possible to climb it, pondering whether there was some way to get to the other side and explore. Sometimes the sun hit it just right so that its reflection off of the pearly sheen became blinding, and Evin found the effect mesmerizing.

But he'd never dared get too close. Everyone knew the wall was magic. It had a way of making people act strangely if they touched it.

Lowering his gaze, Evin climbed to his feet and rubbed at his eyes. "That was a low move," he said to Jorick. "Making me hit the wall doesn't mean you've won. We are going. Tonight."

Jorick didn't respond. Prepared to renew their brawl, Evin lowered his hands and balled them into fists. But Jorick wasn't looking at Evin. Instead, his eyes were aimed at the tree line. His wooden sword lay in the dirt.

The faint smell of ash met Evin's nose and he followed Jorick's line of sight.

A dark column of smoke rose from somewhere beyond the forest.

"The village," Evin whispered.

Chapter Two

Evin and Jorick raced through the trees toward Hesiod. Low-hanging branches slapped their cheeks and they stumbled over bushes, but Evin didn't care.

Marten was there. His mother. All the other people he'd grown up with. And yes, his father, who he now desperately hoped was all right.

As the boys reached the tree line, the flames were so hot that even from across a clearing, the heat warmed their skin. The massive building closest to them—the inn—was already engulfed by fire.

"No!" Evin screamed. Not thinking, he raced to the burning building, sure that he would find his family in a bucket line, working to put out the fire.

But as he got close, he saw the inn wasn't the only building on fire. Every building in the village—from the town hall to the many thatched-roof homes, from the bakery to the stables—was burning. People ran through streets, fleeing from nightmarish creatures brandishing battle-axes. Evin's blood ran cold and his arms began to tremble. He skidded to a stop.

"Why are you stopping?" Jorick shouted, but then he saw the monsters too.

The creatures were taller than any man Evin knew, and though they walked on two legs and held their axes in two muscular arms, they most certainly were not men. What parts of their bodies weren't covered by piecemeal armor were instead covered by mangy, matted yellow fur.

Their heads hung low from the top of their wide torsos, their faces elongated into snouts like a dog's or a wolf's. Their ragged, pointed ears jerked around to catch the sounds of everything around them. Their sharp teeth and yellow eyes glinted, reflecting the flames.

There were dozens of the creatures, surely at least two for each villager who lived in Hesiod. They moved in twos and threes, grabbing and smacking the villagers over their heads, then dragging them north, beyond the burning village. Their cries were high pitched, nasal, and whining—a staccato and unnerving sound almost like mocking laughter.

The monsters weren't eating the villagers. They were kidnapping them, Evin realized. Maybe there was hope. Maybe he and Jorick could stop the creatures and—

A growl sounded from beside Evin. He looked to his side just in time to see Jorick—the source of the growl—begin to run toward the monsters, his hands clenched into fists.

Evin dropped his useless, fake dagger and pumped his arms, running as fast as he could. His calves ached and his lungs burned, but Evin pushed himself through the pain. They had to get to the village. They had to save their families.

It felt like Evin had dived headfirst into an oven as they ran past the collapsing inn. The heat from the flames dried his skin, and smoke invaded his eyes, his throat. He coughed and waved his hand in front of his face, trying to make out through tear-blurred eyes which shadows were people and which were the horrifying monsters.

"Dad!" Jorick screamed. "Dad!" He darted back and forth beside Evin, tears making tracks down his soot-stained cheeks.

Evin's heart thudded. He and Jorick moved deeper into the burning village, scanning for any signs of life. Most of the monsters were gone and the screams were fading, but the boys couldn't give up.

Evin jumped as timber creaked, then thudded beside him. The supports of the town hall gave way and the building fell in on itself.

Then, in front of Evin, someone emerged from the smoke, shielding his face and hacking. For a moment, in his panicked, confused state, Evin almost thought he was looking at his own reflection—the figure was tall, slender, and blond. But then the other boy lowered his arm.

Relief flooded into Evin's tense muscles. "Marten!"

Marten's pale eyes widened. "Evin!"

Evin ran to his brother and barreled into his chest.

"We have to run!" Marten shouted over the din of the crackling flames. "We have to get out of here!"

"Where are Mother and Father?" Evin shouted back.

"Have you seen my dad?" Jorick asked.

"They're gone!" Marten pulled away. "Those creatures took them all. We have to save ourselves now or—"

Jorick cried out and Marten spun around. One of the monsters emerged from the smoke, shadowy and backlit by the flames. It snarled, then opened its jaws and howled, the sound like some vicious laugh.

It raised its axe high, and for a brief, terrifying moment, Evin thought the monster might slice his only brother in two. Instead, the creature brought the flat side of the blade down against Marten's head. There was a sickening, heavy clang and Marten collapsed to the ground. His limbs were slack and bent, like a marionette with its strings cut.

"No!" Evin cried, and the monster's yellow eyes darted up from Marten to look at him. The flames reflected in its pupils, making its eyes look as if they were glowing.

Evin's stomach fell, and he felt as if his legs had turned to string. But when the monster moved as though to come at him, some reserve of strength surged through Evin's aching limbs. He grabbed Jorick by the arm and ran.

They reached the edge of the village, where the cobblestone streets met the now blackened grass. There, gasping for air, Evin finally let go of Jorick's arm.

"We have to leave now," Evin said, his voice trembling. "We have to go back to the woods."

"We can't!" Jorick shouted. "We have to stop those monsters!"

"With what, our fists?"

"If we have to!"

The inn groaned beside them, letting out a final creak as its remaining wall fell. Soot and dust rose. Sparks swirled through the darkness. Coughing, Evin stepped farther back into the clearing, the cool night air soothing the tender, dried skin on his cheeks.

"We're leaving," Evin said. "Everyone is gone. We got here too late. We have to run before those things come after us too!"

Jorick recoiled. "But my dad! And your brother! He—"

"My brother said we have to save ourselves!" Evin shouted. "And . . . and he was right. Now come on!"

Jorick opened his mouth to say something, but he stopped short as the monsters' horrible, howling laughter rose somewhere through the smoke behind them. Without another word, Jorick nodded at Evin. Then, the two boys ran once more—away from the village and back into the woods.

Chapter Three

Rain pattered against the forest canopy. Evin almost couldn't look at the campfire he and Jorick had built. It kept reminding him of home—of his former home, anyway. Memories appeared in his mind then: Just the day before, he'd spent the day working with his father to prepare rooms for the traders from Forestedge who were supposed to be coming in that evening. Just the day before, Marten had given him the little dagger he'd carved, a gift for Evin after he successfully swiped the insufferable assistant mayor's monogrammed handkerchief. Just the day before . . .

It was all gone now. His father and his demands. His mother, who always kept the inn's patrons laughing while she delivered their drinks. Marten and his secret lessons on being a rogue. The inn he'd longed to escape was now nothing but a pile of embers.

But just because the village was gone didn't mean the people who had lived there were gone. The monsters hadn't killed anyone, not that Evin had seen. They had taken them somewhere. Evin could track down the villagers.

Now he'd get to be a hero like he had always wanted.

He sighed. He'd wanted a new life—but not like this. Not at the expense of everyone he ever knew.

Jorick sat on the other side of the fire, his hair soaked with rainwater. His jaw was clenched. The flames cast menacing shadows over his features.

Evin's stomach growled. They needed food. And more important, they needed to figure out where the dog-men had taken their families.

He stood up and wiped the mud from his trousers as best he could. He kicked dirt onto the fire, dousing most of the flames.

Jorick leaped to his feet. "Is it time?" he asked. "You think it's been long enough?"

Searching through the nearby brush for a broken branch that was mostly dry, Evin nodded. "The fires are probably out by now, and those creatures are gone. We should go see what's left."

Jorick narrowed his eyes. "You kept us waiting so that we could scavenge? I thought you were just trying to keep us alive so we could go rescue them. I know you hated your dad, but I'm not letting mine get eaten by monsters."

"I won't either!" Evin said. "Of course we're going after them. But first we need supplies . . ."—he hesitated, then added in a quiet voice—"and I didn't hate my father."

14

Jorick stomped past Evin into the trees and toward the village. "If you say so."

Evin put the tip of the branch he had found into the dying fire and let it light, then kicked dirt over the rest of the campfire and followed Jorick through the trees.

When he reached the tree line, Evin saw the remnants of Hesiod. The village had transformed into a shadowy ruin of jagged black planks, crumbled stone walls, and soot-stained rubble. Jorick was already climbing through the remains of the razed buildings, barely visible in what little moonlight shone between the clouds.

Evin could feel tears burning at his eyes. But he needed to keep up a brave face, if only to keep Jorick calm. Swallowing the lump in his throat, he followed Jorick into the village.

The rain had been more than heavy enough earlier in the evening to melt the smoldering ash into the dirt. The result was a slick slurry that squished around Evin's boots as he walked the narrow streets of what had once been his home. He felt empty as he looked at the shells of the buildings, their insides hollowed out by the dog-men's blaze. He half hoped that he'd find someone hiding in the buildings that weren't all the way burned down. Maybe Marten had escaped and was waiting to meet up with him.

But the buildings were empty. The monsters had taken every last villager. Aside from the patter of the drizzling rain, the once bustling streets of Hesiod were completely silent.

Evin caught up to Jorick in what used to be the town square. Jorick was staring at the destroyed blacksmith shop that had belonged to his father. His breaths were ragged.

For a long moment, Jorick didn't say anything. "So, Evin," he finally whispered. "What do we do first?"

"Well," Evin whispered back, "before we go after those creatures, we need to be ready. Maybe . . . maybe some weapons? Real ones, not wooden ones."

Jorick grunted and headed toward the rubble. Evin ducked beneath a broken beam. The air smelled thick and smoky, and Evin felt almost as if the acrid paste of ash and dirt were coating his throat.

He held the small torch high as they looked around the blacksmith shop's ruined floor. Metal clanked against metal as their boots hit soot-stained tools that had fallen from their places on the walls and were now scattered into the dirt. It actually seemed that most of the metal instruments were intact—the flames hadn't had a chance to grow hot enough to melt them before the rain began to fall.

Evin found a short sword hidden beneath the muddy ash, and a pair of daggers nearby. He tucked them all between his belt and his waist. The metal bit into his side. Meanwhile Jorick cursed as he tossed through the rubble, even kicking at the massive anvil that still stood proudly in the corner.

"Hey, I know it's bad, but we'll save them," Evin said. "I know we will."

"It's not that. I just need . . . here!"

Jorick dived into the rubble and began digging. He emerged a moment later brandishing a sword, his cheeks stained with soot. It was apparent from the ornate hilt and the reverent way Jorick held the weapon that this was no ordinary sword.

Jorick swung it through the air in two slashing motions, his muscles tensing with the weight even though working the sword seemed natural to him. For the first time in hours, a broad grin spread across Jorick's dirty face.

"My dad's sword," he said. Meeting Evin's eyes, he expertly swirled the sword one last time and then shoved it through his belt. "He said this was the best balanced sword he ever made and that when I was ready, it would be mine."

Evin nodded. "And now it is. I bet he knows you're going to come for him."

"Yeah." Jorick looked down at his muddy feet.

Evin was about to speak again when both boys heard a heavy thudding nearby and a high-pitched voice say something, the words muffled.

Evin stiffened, his hand flying to the weapon at his side. He put his hand on Jorick's shoulder and then put his finger to his lips. Jorick nodded and together they tiptoed out of the building, straining to hear where the noise had come from.

Another thud. Another muffled, high-pitched curse.

Evin looked at Jorick and mouthed, "The mayor's storehouse." Jorick nodded, his eyes flashing from the torchlight.

As they grew closer, the sounds of something scrabbling through the rubble grew louder. The stone walls of the mayor's personal storehouse were surprisingly intact—in fact, the building appeared to be one of the few to have been mostly spared from the raging fires, with only its roof really burned away. Meanwhile the mayor's former residence, which had once stood beside the storehouse, was completely decimated, nothing but rubble anymore.

Evin gestured toward the storehouse's doorway with his head and the boys took up position on either side, their backs pressed against the wet stone. Evin strained to listen. It didn't seem to be more than one creature. Could it be one of the dog-men? If it was, now it would get a chance to feel as terrified as Evin had felt earlier.

With a nod from Evin, Jorick brandished his sword and dived into the store, screaming. Evin did the same, raising his sword and waving it around as he shouted.

Evin skid to a stop as he entered the building, almost falling in the mud. For a moment, he and Jorick stood side by side, hollering until their voices were hoarse, hoping to frighten whoever or whatever was inside with them. Finally they needed to catch their breath, and only then did Evin make out what it was that had been scavenging through the storeroom's toppled shelves.

The creature—the person, actually—was an old woman even shorter than Jorick. A strange smell wafted off of her, something musty and earthy and strangely familiar, though Evin couldn't remember if he'd ever seen her about town before. She parted her thin lips, revealing a mouth of stained yellow teeth—what teeth there were left, anyway. Clucking, she shook her head.

"Kids today," she croaked. "Hooligans, the lot of you. Always bothering me while I do my shopping."

Evin and Jorick stood still, their swords raised high and their mouths slack. The old woman shoved between them, studied the jars that lay shattered over the floor, and resumed digging through the mayor's supplies.

Chapter Four

Evin blinked as he watched the old woman dig through the rubble and place items in her apron as though oblivious to the destruction around her or the fact that it was quite dark and difficult to see.

After a moment, he cleared his throat. "Um, excuse me."

The woman ignored him, choosing instead to peer intently inside a barrel full of pickles.

"Excuse me, ma'am," Evin said, louder this time. Beside him, Jorick still looked on slack jawed.

The woman stuck one gnarled hand into the barrel's briny water, pulled out a pickle, sniffed it, and dropped it in the folds of her apron.

Finally, Jorick regained his bearings. Brow furrowed, he took two heavy steps forward and gripped the woman firmly by her arm. "Hey!" he said. "My friend is talking to you, la—whoa!"

Green sparks burst from the woman's arm and Jorick reeled backward. As he lost control of his sword, the weight of the weapon threw him off balance and he fell on his backside.

The old woman turned on the two boys, a spindly, knotted finger held high. She looked between them with her eerily yellow eyes slitted.

"I told you two ruffians," she said in her raspy, frog-like voice, "I need to do my shopping! I haven't time to discipline two unbridled lads who haven't learned to mind their elders. Gods forbid a day go by without one of you lot trying to ruin my day!"

"But . . ." Evin stammered, "ma'am, it's night. Monsters have taken all of the villagers. The entire village has been burned down and this isn't a shop, it's a storehouse. Didn't . . . didn't you notice?"

The woman's finger stopped midwag and she raised one of her molting eyebrows. She looked up at the wide-open space above her where the storehouse's roof used to be.

"Hmm," she said. "I was wondering why it was so quiet around here, and so messy. Well, no matter. Doesn't change the fact I need to stock up for the week." With a shrug of her shoulders, the woman turned around and once again resumed ransacking the shelves.

By now, Jorick had stood up from where he'd fallen. It was dark, but Evin could clearly see his friend's clenched jaw. Before Evin could stop him, Jorick stepped right up to the old woman one more time, though now he knew better than to touch her.

"You're crazy, you old bat!" he shouted. "My dad was kidnapped! My home was burned down by monsters! And all you care about is completing your shopping list?" Jorick shook his head angrily and brandished his sword in front of him. "I bet you're in on it, aren't you? You have magic, I saw it. You're a witch! I bet you helped those dog-men raid the village so you could come ransack it!"

"I did no such thing," the woman grumbled as she wiped wet ash off an unshattered jar of apricot preserves.

"Liar!" Jorick screamed. He looked about ready to slice the woman in two. Before he could, Evin leaped forward and placed a gentle hand on Jorick's tensed arm.

"Jorick, no," he said as calmly as he could. "I don't think she helped the dog-men. But I bet she could help us. I think you're right—she's a witch. I think I've seen her before."

At that, the old woman ceased bustling around the messy shop. Slowly she turned her squat body around to face them, then smiled her gap-toothed smile at Evin.

"Seen me before, have you?" she croaked. "Who exactly do you think I am?"

Evin swallowed and lowered his hand from Jorick's arm. "The Swamp Witch," he said. "When Jorick called you a witch I remembered where I smelled you before."

The woman let out a creaky laugh. "Smelled me? Well aren't you a charmer."

Evin smiled uneasily. "No, just, it's a distinctive smell—like the swampland. I went there once, when I was younger. I followed the wall through the forest south of here."

The story bubbled into Evin's mind, the memories of his trek to discover the end of the giant white wall were suddenly so distinctive it was as though it had happened yesterday.

"I didn't get far because I ran into swampland," Evin continued, "and that's a particular smell you don't forget. I saw a house there and asked my father about it later, and he told me that a woman lived there. The Swamp Witch. Not two days later I smelled the swamp again in town, and saw, well, you."

The old woman laughed again. "I'm famous! Who would have thought?"

Though still tense and breathing heavily with anger, Jorick lowered his sword. "So I was right. You are a witch."

The woman nodded. "That I am," she said. "And you're lucky I don't turn you two into boils and add you to the collection on my underarm."

"Lucky!" Jorick bellowed. "Why I ought to—"

Again Evin grabbed Jorick's arm, and his friend went silent. The Swamp Witch looked between the two of them, amused.

"So you say the village was burned down?" she croaked. "By dog-men? Hmm. Interesting."

Before Jorick could snap at the woman again, Evin stepped in front of him and nodded. The woman was most certainly strange and more than a little off-putting, but she was an adult, and a witch to boot. He decided to play along and see if she could do anything for them.

"Yes. I guess since it's, um, dark you might be able to miss it."

Her thin lips spread into a wide, toady grin. "Perhaps."

The woman tightened the knot of the kerchief covering her wispy white hair.

Evin cleared his throat. Behind him, Jorick's hot, snorting breaths lashed against Evin's neck.

Finally, the old woman sighed and threw her hands into the air. "I suppose you two aren't going to stop bothering me unless I help you?"

"That would be quite kind of you, ma'am," Evin said.

The Swamp Witch put one hand on her hip and jabbed Evin in the chest with the index finger of her other hand. "You ever go adventuring, boy? Aside from following the wall and sneaking up to my house?"

Evin shook his head. "No, ma'am. But I sure think I'd be able to. I've been preparing for years and years."

"You know how to use those weapons you got?"

"Yes, ma'am," Evin said. "Well . . . sort of. We practice a lot with, um, wooden ones."

"Of course we know how to use weapons," Jorick called from behind Evin. "What do you think we are? Kids?"

The Swamp Witch guffawed, the sound halfway between a bark and a belch. "Oh, of course not! I daresay you two are strapping young warriors, ready for oodles of battles." Stepping back from Evin, the old woman turned, bent over, and peered at the grain sacks on the bottom of a nearby undestroyed shelf. Evin and Jorick waited expectantly.

The Swamp Witch shopped.

"Um, excuse me, ma'am," Evin said after a long moment, doing his best to hide the irritation in his voice. "About that help?"

The Swamp Witch turned around and rolled her yellow eyes. "You two still here? Blast. I thought I might be able to trick you into leaving me be. Fine, fine." Beckoning with a gnarled finger, she gestured for the boys to come close.

Evin and Jorick leaned in. The woman's swampy stench was overwhelming, drowning out the smell of the ash and mud.

"You two ever hear of a wizard named Zendric?" the witch asked. "He lived in the old city of Curston. Perhaps you know of it?"

It took Evin a moment, but the memories bubbled of such a place—ruins of a great city that lay north of Hesiod. "Yes," he said, "we know the place."

"Well, Zendric was a foremost expert on monsters," the Swamp Witch went on. "Not that I doubt your amazing prowess in battle, but I daresay that if you want to find and fight these 'dog-men' and save your townspeople, Zendric is your wizard."

Evin leaned back and smiled. Suddenly their quest to find the dog-men didn't seem so impossible. "The wizard Zendric," he said. "And Curston. Got it."

"Good," the old woman said, then adjusted the kerchief around her wrinkled face. "Now, seriously lads, leave me alone. You're making my third eye twitch."

Jorick's forehead crinkled. "Your third . . . What?"

But the old woman had resumed ignoring them, bustling across the sludge-covered ground to continue her shopping.

Brow still furrowed, Jorick looked up at Evin. "Do you really think we can trust that woman?" he whispered. "She's totally crazy!"

Evin bit his lip. "Well, I don't know what else we

can do. We don't really have any other plan, and Curston isn't far. A wizard who's an expert on monsters would be really helpful."

"Are you sure?" Jorick asked. "I just remembered that my dad took me to Curston once. That place is in total ruins. There's nothing there. Why would some famous wizard live there?"

Evin shrugged. "I have no idea. But we have to try if we want to save our families."

Jorick looked down and his voice fell. "You think if we do this, we'll find my dad?"

"I'm sure of it. We go to Curston, and then we'll find your dad, all right?"

Jorick glanced up and watched the Swamp Witch croak in glee upon discovering a jar of dried chickens' feet.

"All right," Jorick said. "But first can we find some food before that witch takes it all?"

Chapter Five

Evin and Jorick salvaged as many food supplies as they could from the mayor's storehouse and the few homes that weren't completely decimated, and retreated back into the woods to sleep. They were both overcome with exhaustion after the long day, and with the clouds covering the night sky it had proven far too dark to travel.

Lying on hard-packed dirt and with rocks digging into his side, Evin thought he'd never get to sleep. Soon, however, he found himself dozing off, his discomfort forgotten in his exhaustion.

Evin dreamed that he was in a giant broken-down house. At first he thought it was the inn, but the building was in too much squalor, and it stank. His parents would never let the inn fall into such disrepair.

In the dream, Evin walked through the halls of giant house, looking through open doorways. There were many other kids huddled in cramped rooms, from babies to teenagers, all wearing worn-out clothes and grumbling about their hunger. Everything seemed gray, and he felt a dreadful sense of unease.

Evin looked out the window of the house and saw the wall that rose from the forest near his village. It was as stark white and never ending as it had seemed that morning when he was awake—only, the wall was different somehow. Its angles, the way it refracted the light, everything about it was different.

Evin hated the house. The walls seemed as though they might fall at any moment and crush him. He wanted to run away, leave the giant house, explore the world.

The dream felt so real—the chill air breaching his thin clothes, the body odor of the other children, the grumbling of his stomach, the longing to be anywhere else in the world—that when Evin woke with sun piercing his eyes, he was confused as to where he was and why he was there.

He rolled onto his back and winced as a particularly large stone cut into the small of his back. He saw the canopy of the trees above him, wet leaves glistening in the sunlight.

Craning his neck back, Evin looked behind him and saw the wall. It was right by the forest, where it always was. It did not look angled improperly and it was the right color.

A boot hit Evin lightly in his side. He rolled his head and looked up. Jorick stood above him, his hair even messier than usual.

"Is it time to go yet?" Jorick asked.

After a quick meal, they gathered their belongings and headed off. They exited the woods to walk around the ruins of Hesiod first, and managed to find traces of tracks from the dog-men. The tracks, too, headed north—the same direction in which Curston lay—and Evin felt sure that it was fate leading them to Zendric now. The wizard would help and everything would be all right.

A wide dirt road cut through the overgrown fields to the north, and Evin and Jorick hiked along it, kicking at stones and saying very little. By midmorning they reached a fork in the road, with the well-traveled path heading east and the path that continued on north to Curston over- grown with towering weeds and thorny vines.

The two boys stomped over the underbrush and went on. Evin felt for a moment like he was heading into the deep wilderness on the grand adventure he'd always wanted—which, he supposed, he was. Even with his worry about his family, Evin felt a strange little thrill. As horrifying as it was to see Hesiod go down in flames, life was now never going to just be the same boring routine every day.

The memory of his dream came back to him. He decided it was probably a dream-twisted vision of his life in the inn. The surroundings hadn't been quite the same, but the feelings of longing to run away most certainly were. In any case, it didn't matter. Now he would never have to go back to the inn—especially after saving his father and proving once and for all that the life of an adventurer was his true destiny.

Curston had long ago been a huge, sprawling mess of buildings separated by wide cobblestone streets and surrounded by towering walls. Evin and Jorick entered the city from the south, which had once been Curston's most expensive—and most elaborate—district. But now the walls and buildings had crumbled into jagged boulders, and wild grass and spindly trees burst up from beneath the cracked cobblestone.

It was quiet in the ruins as Evin and Jorick crept past a fallen stone dome and broken arches. A soft breeze brushed past them, rustling flowers and grass in a gentle, soothing manner. Above, the serious storm clouds of the night before had departed, leaving behind friendly puffs that swam in the blue expanse of spring sky.

Jorick kicked at the trunk of a willow tree whose long branches swayed in the breeze like a maiden's hair. His sword was drawn, and a scowl creased his face.

"It's quiet here," Jorick grumbled. "And pretty."

Evin went up to his friend's side and set down their sack of food. "I know. Isn't it nice? I can't believe I ever used to be afraid to come up here, all those old stories of this being the 'Cursed Town' and all."

Jorick looked up at Evin and shook his head. "No, I mean it," he said. "It's too quiet. And too pretty. I don't trust this place."

Evin laughed. "What could possibly be bad about—" To the northeast, something cracked, a sound loud like thunder.

"—this place," Evin finished.

Jorick pushed aside the boughs of the willow tree. "What was that? The dog-men?"

"I don't think so." Shading his eyes from the midday sun, Evin looked toward the origin of the sound. He scanned the ground, following the remnants of old roads and ruined buildings. Everything looked mostly the same—until he saw the tower.

How had he not noticed the tower until now? There it was, plain and clear: a round column rising the height of ten men into the sky, with a pointed, shingled roof.

Despite being surrounded by a destroyed ancient city, the tower seemed almost new.

"Look!" Evin said, grabbing Jorick's tensed arm in excitement. "That's it. It has to be Zendric's tower. We're almost there!"

"What about the noise?" Jorick asked. "Maybe the dog-men got here first."

Evin grinned, picked up the food sack, and began to head down what was once the main cobblestone street that ran through Curston's wealthiest district. "Probably just some wizard experiments. You know what they always say about magic-users and their studies."

Evin stopped and turned around when he realized Jorick hadn't moved from his spot near the willow tree. The shorter boy looked up at the distant tower with suspicion.

"Come on," Evin called back. "Your dad's waiting for you to save him!"

Shaking his head as though breaking out of a stupor, Jorick sheathed his sword. "Coming!"

Together the boys ran north, following the old road since the wilderness and fallen buildings made making a beeline to the tower an unwise plan. In the center of the ruins lay a wide clearing that must have once been the town square. On the western edge of the square lay the crumbling remains of what must have once been a church, what with the fallen flying buttresses and bits of colored glass lying about. Part of an old, circled cross lay splayed across the overgrown main square.

Evin led the way from that point, veering right and heading east down another barely visible old street. The building remains in this new section of old Curston were decidedly less classic than those of the rich quarter they'd trudged through earlier. The bits of old architecture still visible were unusual and spindly in ways Evin had never before seen. Surely this part of town must have been for the more unique citizens. Evin wondered what lay hidden beneath the rubble. Ancient magic relics? Buried treasures? He decided to come back and explore the city once the villagers were saved.

Finally, after climbing over fallen walls and rounding a forest of trees, Evin and Jorick reached the base of the unusually pristine tower.

It seemed even larger now that they were so close. Looking up at its roof, Evin felt dizzy, as if he might fall over from trying to take in the immensity of it all. There were no cracks in the stone that made up its round walls, no vines snaked up its side. A small white house stood attached to the base.

"Now what?" Jorick asked. His giant sword gestured to the house's red door. "Should I kick it down?"

"I think," Evin said, "that maybe we should try knocking."

"What about that noise we heard?" Jorick asked. "This guy could be dangerous."

Evin winked at his friend. "All the more reason not to startle him."

He strode to the door and rapped against it three times. After a moment with no answer, he called out, "Hello? Master Zendric? Are you home? We need your help!"

Another long moment. Still no answer.

Jorick came to Evin's side. He put his hand on his hip and said, "Something isn't right. We heard noises coming from here, so we know he's inside."

Evin shrugged. "Maybe he needs to straighten up before receiving guests."

Jorick banged against the door with the side of his fist. "Open up! I know you're in there!"

"Hey!" Evin said. "Don't do that. You'll make him mad."

Jorick glared at Evin. He hesitated for a moment, then banged once more with his fist. The door rattled in its frame.

Still no answer.

Jorick shoved his sleeves up his forearms. "That's it, now I'm kicking it down."

Before Evin could object and before Jorick could move, there came the sound of another loud crack. At the same time, in a flash of orange light and an explosion of shimmering smoke, the door burst open and slammed against the side of the house.

In the doorway stood the most beautiful girl Evin had ever seen. The girl tapped her foot, arms crossed and her pointed chin held high.

"No one," she said, "is going to break down any doors. Now, tell me who you are and what you want, or else I'll be the one doing the kicking around here."

Chapter Six

Before Evin could stop him, Jorick leaped forward and grabbed the girl's arm. "Hey, listen, I—"

Jorick didn't get a chance to finish his sentence. He flew backward in a shower of orange sparks, landed on his backside on the broken cobblestone street, and sat there, stunned.

The girl shrugged. "I warned you."

Evin stifled a grin. He couldn't help but feel Jorick deserved to end up on his backside after he had ignored his advice yet again.

The girl arched an eyebrow at Evin. "Well? Were you banging on my door for a reason or did you just come to disrupt my studies?"

Smiling in the way his mother had always told him was so terribly charming, Evin stepped around Jorick and bowed his head.

"My apologies for my friend's rude behavior," he said, then looked up into her eyes. They were so blue that they seemed as deep and mysterious as the ocean. "My name is Evin, and this is Jorick. We were told to come here to find the wizard Zendric. See, our village, Hesiod, was—"

"Zendric?" the girl interrupted, raising her other eyebrow.

Evin nodded. "Yes, see, our village was burned down by these dog-men, and they kidnapped everyone. There was an old witch who came to, erm, shop in the evening. She told us that the wizard Zendric lived here and that, what with him being a world-renowned expert on monsters, we should come talk to him so he can help us save our people."

"Sorry, he can't help you." The girl shook her head, sending her copper hair shimmering over her shoulders. "He's not here." With a wave of her slender finger, the door began to creak close.

"Wait!" Evin cried, then jumped forward to the grab the door before it could shut all the way. "Please, it's important, the dog-men—"

Inside, the girl said, "Gnolls."

"Excuse me?" Evin asked. He blinked, trying to clear his eyes of daylight so as to see inside. It remained shrouded in shadow.

Then, the girl was in front of him, standing nose to nose and eye to eye. " 'Dog-men' is not the correct term for the creatures who took your friends. They're called gnolls."

"Gnolls," Evin repeated, unable to unlock his eyes from the girl's.

"That's right. Gnolls. Cackling, ubiquitous, dumb hordes driven by hunger. Too cowardly to hunt alone, they are mostly found in packs. They like to eat people because they scream more." She waved her hands in the air as though presenting something. "Gnolls."

The girl relayed the information as though she'd had to recite it before, in the same way Evin's father made him repeat the family recipe for mulled wine when he was younger.

"Oh, all right," Evin said. "So, these gnolls like to . . . eat people?"

The girl nodded. "Yes, they usually pounce upon them, eat their fill, and leave the carcasses to the scavenger birds. Really, I'm surprised someone from a place so close to Curston as Hesiod has never heard of gnolls. That's like saying you've never heard of goblins. They're everywhere, and they're rather annoying."

Evin shrugged. "We never had any gnolls or other monsters come near our town. Not that I know of, anyway."

The girl looked Evin up and down, then crossed her arms. "Gnolls took your people and you're off to find them, and you know nothing about the creatures?" She shook her head. "No wonder the witch sent you here. You're totally clueless."

Evin bristled at that, but he kept his smile plastered on his face. "Well, can you clue us in?"

The girl shoved her hair behind her pointed ears, then put her delicate hands on her hips. It was then that Evin realized this girl, this wizard, was an elf. Evin had never seen an elf before, but he'd heard of them. Elves were notorious for their ethereal beauty, as well as their complete and utter snobbishness. So far, it seemed she quite lived up to the stereotype.

Sighing, the elf girl walked back into the darkness of the tower. Her white robe embroidered with intricate, runic patterns swirled around her feet. She turned back to look at Evin. "Come on, then. And bring your angry little friend too."

"Thank you!" Evin said. "Thank you very much!"

From the depths of the tower, the girl called out, "Hurry before I change my mind."

Evin left the door halfway open, spun around, and bounded to where Jorick still sat in the dirt and weeds.

Jorick climbed to his feet. "That is the second time in a day that some witch has thrown me to the ground with magic," he said. "I'm beginning to hate magic-users."

Evin slapped his friend on the back. "I told you not to go banging on someone's door like that. And at least this witch is a whole lot better looking than the last one."

"Wizard."

Startled, Evin looked up. The elf girl stood once more in the doorway. Heat rushed to his cheeks.

"Witches do their creepy spells without any regard to the theorems of magic and are, in general, incredibly disgusting hags." Her hand fluttered to her chest and she raised her narrow chin. "I am a scholar of magic who takes pride in her work. There is a difference."

"Wait till she's old and wrinkled, then try and tell me she's any different," Jorick muttered.

Evin ignored him. Despite the girl's condescension and bossiness, he needed her help. "Sorry. No offense."

The girl shrugged. "Common mistake. Now get in here, we're letting in a draft."

Chapter Seven

For a moment, Evin stood in the darkness, suddenly unsure of whether he should trust a magic-using girl whose name he didn't even know, no matter how pretty she was. Then, the girl muttered a word, and a warm glow filled their surroundings.

Evin found himself at the entrance to a library that was far more vast than he would have thought from outside. In fact, he was quite sure it shouldn't have been physically possible for a room this wide and this tall to exist inside the small building they'd entered.

Shelves made of dark, polished, and carved wood lined every wall, and towering bookcases were set in three rows through the center of the room. At one end of the stacks sat two plush chairs and a short marble table. Glass orbs filled with light hovered overhead.

Hundreds, if not thousands, of leather-bound books lined the shelves. The musky smell of aging parchment met Evin's nose. Here and there on the shelves, between the tomes, sat unusual, foreign artifacts that Evin was sure must be magic: statues vaguely shaped like humans, crystal balls, gems the size of his fists, animal claws the size of his head.

The girl stepped in front of Evin and Jorick. "This is Boccob Library." She gestured around her with a long, spindly wand that she now clutched in her right hand. The wand's wooden shaft was dark and polished, with runic symbols carved into it, and decorated with raised images of birds in flight. At the base of the wand, a round, green gem cast a gentle glow. "It is rare that any non-magic-user is ever allowed in here, but I can't very well send you two off to fight gnolls unprepared."

"Gnolls?" Jorick asked. "What are you talking about? We're looking for dog-men."

The girl sighed, then repeated word for word what she'd told Evin about the gnolls. He was right. She had recited it before.

Jorick's eyes grew wider and wider. After the last bit about gnolls eating humans, he recoiled.

"They really are going to eat everyone? Are you serious?" He spun around and grabbed Evin by the shoulders. "Evin, we've really got to go now! We can't waste our time in libraries with weird elves!"

"Weird?" the girl said, her voice rising.

Jorick turned to her. "Well you are! Doing your

light show and acting all mysterious. We don't even know your name."

The girl sniffed and crossed her arms.

Jorick snorted and shoved past the girl to head deeper into the library. "It doesn't matter anyway. Evin said that when we find this Zendric person, he's going to help us kill all the gnolls and then we're going to save everyone." Placing his hands around his mouth, Jorick called out, "Zendric! Hey, Zendric!"

"I told you!" the girl said, her voice sharp and loud. "He's not here."

Jorick spun to face her. "Well where is he, then? We need to hurry! Everyone is going to die!" Throwing his hands up in the air, Jorick slumped into one of the plush chairs. "Can anyone tell me why everyone in the world has gone crazy since yesterday? My best friend makes me let my dad get taken by gnolls, a batty old witch goes shopping in smoldering ruins in the dead of night, and now this elf girl wants to act all snooty and, yes, weird." Jorick slammed his fists against the chair's armrests. "You are all insane!"

The last words of Jorick's rant echoed between the distant, unseen rafters of the library as all three fell quiet. Evin felt a pang deep in his chest.

"I didn't make you leave anyone behind," Evin

said. "You heard Marten. Those gnolls had already taken everyone. We needed to save ourselves so we could save them."

Jorick glared at Evin. "You didn't even try to save your brother. You just ran. He was lying there and we left him."

"I . . ." Evin didn't know what to say. It was true. But he'd only been doing what was best: running and hiding and living to fight another day.

He remembered Marten lying on the soot-stained cobblestones, motionless, with the salivating gnoll hunched over him. He remembered the heat of the flames threatening to engulf them. He'd been so scared. Maybe he should have fought back his fear rather than run away. He didn't know anymore.

"My name is Betilivatis."

Evin jerked his head and looked over at the elf.

"I am a wizard's apprentice," she went on. "Zendric was my master. He . . . he disappeared, many years ago, on some quest he refused to talk about. I come here all the time, hoping to find him, but he's never here. So while I wait for Zendric's return, I read his books and I teach myself what I need to know." Looking between Evin and the scowling Jorick, her eyes seemed friendly and concerned. "I'm not the monster expert Zendric is, but . . . maybe I can help you save your families."

Betilivatis swept past Jorick and headed down the corridor between two rows of bookshelves. Her white robes rustled behind her as she traced her fingers along the bindings of the many tomes set on the shelves, her eyes scanning the unusual words. Finally she stopped, her thin lips briefly curling into a smile. She slipped her wand inside the folds of her robe, then pulled a book from the shelf.

Armed with a book bound in green leather, Betilivatis rushed back down the aisle to where the boys were. She held it up for both to look at, and Evin read the title to himself: *A Practical Guide to Monsters.* Embedded in its cover was a painting of a strange creature with three monstrous heads and a pair of red, batlike wings.

"If you're going to head out to hunt monsters and save your village," Betilivatis went on, "you're going to need this. Before Zendric disappeared, he left this behind for his apprentices. It contains his writings on monsters you may encounter and how to fight—or flee—from them."

Betilivatis sat in a chair opposite Jorick and rested the book in her lap. "I have a theory about these gnolls and the villagers. I don't think the gnolls have eaten anyone."

Jorick sat up. "You don't? You think we can save them?" In his voice lay the faintest sound of hope.

Betilivatis nodded. "Like I said before, gnolls have an insatiable hunger. Typically they attack their victims as a pack, eat them, and leave. They certainly don't take whole villages captive, especially without even leaving one dead body behind." She leaned forward and placed her elbows on her knees. "I would venture to theorize that the gnolls are working for someone—or something—who wanted those people taken alive."

Evin kneeled beside Jorick's chair and gripped his friend's shoulder reassuringly. "That's great!" he said to Betilivatis. "Then we can track down the gnolls and free everyone."

Betilivatis smiled. "Gnolls often make alliances with other creatures." She lifted up the book in her lap. "And I'm willing to bet that one of the monsters Zendric wrote about has become their leader."

"Wonderful!" Evin stood and put his hand on the book. "Well, then give us the book and we'll be on our way. We can't wait for—"

Betilivatis jerked the book back. "This book cannot leave my possession," she said.

Jorick scowled and leaped from his chair. Before he could shout more rants into the library's rafters, Evin placed his hand on his friend's shoulder.

"Well, thank you for the information you could give us, Betilivatis," he said. "We really appreciate it, don't we, Jorick?"

Jorick kicked at the hard wood floor.

"But I don't understand why you'd say we need the book and then not let us borrow it," Evin went on. "If what you say about gnolls is true, I don't think that whoever they've allied with can keep them in check for much longer. They could start eating the villagers any moment now and we need to hurry."

Betilivatis leaned back, crossed her legs, and steepled her slender fingers in front of her face.

"Like I said earlier, you two haven't the first idea what you're doing," she said. "Rushing out to face a monstrous horde with even less sense than you have weapons."

Slowly, Betilivatis rose from the chair to tower over Jorick and stand eye to eye with Evin. "It's been boring in this tower all these years," she went on. "And I could really use some field practice with my magic."

"And what does that mean?" Jorick asked.

Betilivatis leaned forward and patted Jorick on the cheek.

"It means," she said, "that I'm coming with you."

Chapter Eight

"G *nolls enmur fawel upwo.*"

Betilivatis stood atop a boulder near the fallen northern gate of Curston. As she spoke the strange words of magic, she pointed the tip of her wand at the ground and let blue sand fall from between her fingers.

The sand snaked through the air and hovered above the swaying grass of the northern plains. It swept above the undulating weeds, as though searching. Then finally, it stopped swirling and fell to the earth. Where it landed, a soft blue glow emanated among the blades of grass.

Brushing away the remaining sand in her hands, Betilivatis spun around to face Evin and Jorick.

"There," she said. "That's our trail. The gnolls appear to have stomped through Curston and kept on heading north."

"Impressive!" Evin offered Betilivatis a hand off the boulder. She accepted with a grudging smile, then hopped down. "Do you think you could show me how to do that?" Evin continued.

"No." Betilivatis turned her back to him and collected her supplies from where they lay spread out on the boulder. She placed the vial of blue sand back inside a leather satchel that she had filled with many other magic supplies and books, including Zendric's *A Practical Guide to Monsters.*

Evin scowled despite himself.

Betilivatis sighed. "Wizardry isn't just a bunch of parlor tricks. It takes years of study. So no, I can't just show you how to do it."

Jorick grunted behind them. Evin looked over his shoulder to see his friend heft their food sack over his shoulder.

"Big deal," Jorick said as he came to their side. "So you can make the ground glow. My dad took me hunting once and he can track just by looking at the way the grass is broken." He turned away from Betilivatis and smirked at Evin. "No need for any magical mumbo jumbo like Bet's."

The girl stiffened. "My proper name," she said as she pulled the strap of her satchel over her shoulder, "is Betilivatis Shandeleynar. And as your father isn't here, my magic tracking will have to do."

Jorick began to weave through the yellow grass, following the faint blue glow. "Yeah, whatever you say, Bet."

The girl snorted, but made no further comment.

"Sorry about that," Evin said. "He shortens everyone's name. He doesn't mean anything by it. He started calling me Evin instead of Evindol, and now everyone does. I actually kind of like it better."

"Yes, well, I don't." Betilivatis motioned forward with her head. "Let's go."

Evin shrugged and jogged past her to walk at Jorick's side.

"I know she's kind of bossy," he whispered in his friend's ear, "but you should be nicer. She doesn't have to help us, and she knows it. We need that book, and if you make her mad enough she'll leave and take it with her."

Jorick adjusted the food sack and glanced up at Evin. "Yeah, I know," he said. "But she shouldn't be coming with us anyway. If she'd just let you have the blasted book, we wouldn't need someone like her following us around."

Evin tilted his head. "Someone like what?"

Jorick hopped over a small boulder in his path. He landed on the glowing trail and sent little bits of the sand flowing around his feet. He took another step, then stumbled, catching himself before he fell.

"She's an elf," he said. "An elf girl. An elf girl wizard.

Any one of those traits by themselves is bad enough, but put them all together?" Jorick shook his head, sending his shaggy brown hair waving. "What we've got is a snobby, know-it-all, purposefully mysterious, possibly dangerous person following us around who is probably going to make a mess of this whole thing. It's bad enough we have to go into a den of monsters without having to worry about her sending fire flying around, or whatever it is she does."

Evin looked back at Betilivatis. The girl's face seemed calm if stern as she followed them. As they walked, the blue trail behind her flew up and disappeared inside her satchel, as though the vial inside were sucking back up the sand.

Evin turned back to his friend. "Well, yes, we don't know much about her yet," he said as they veered their course to walk around a cluster of trees. "But I say we should use her help as long as we can. Her magic will come in handy in a fight."

Jorick opened his mouth to speak but once again tripped over his feet. He grabbed onto Evin's arm to steady himself. "Sorry," he muttered as he righted himself and resumed following the blue trail through the grass. "Anyway, I just don't trust magic. Spending your whole life by yourself, reading books to learn how to control things you shouldn't be able to control . . . it's just creepy, that's all."

Evin smirked. "What do you trust, then?"

Jorick patted the sword at his side. "Steel. Man-made, perfectly natural steel. Like my dad always says, a man is . . . whoa!"

Once more Jorick stumbled over his feet. This time, there was no catching himself. Jorick pinwheeled his arms as he tried to regain his balance, letting the food sack fall to the ground. But it was no use. He lurched forward and fell face first into the dirt.

"Everything all right up there?"

Evin looked over his shoulder to see Betilivatis stopped behind them, her hand held high in the air and a smile on her face. Seeing Evin staring at her, she shot her hand to her side and adjusted her look to one of concern.

Spitting dirt and grass from between his lips, Jorick sat up and looked back, face red with embarrassment. "Yeah," he said. "Just clumsy I guess."

"Well, be more careful," Betilivatis said as she resumed following the trail. As she passed Jorick where he sat in the grass brushing the dirt off his shirt, she glanced down at him over her nose. "Wouldn't want you falling and accidentally impaling yourself on that trusty, man-made, perfectly natural steel sword."

With that, Betilivatis walked on, the bits of blue dust continuing to swirl into her satchel as she passed.

Jorick got to his feet and picked up the food sack. "See," he muttered to Evin as the two boys followed Betilivatis and her magic trail. "Creepy."

Evin watched Bet forge ahead. "Yes," he agreed. "She's definitely strange."

The trio reached the trail's end as the sun began its westward descent behind the great white wall. What they found was another set of ruins, even older than those at Curston. A small river cut a path through the middle of the ruins, from east to west. The water crested and formed waterfalls over buildings that had collapsed into the riverbed.

As the last bits of blue sand disappeared into Betilivatis's vial, the girl put her hands on her hips, pursed her lips, and surveyed the crumbling pillars and churning water before them.

"The tracks stop here," she announced as Evin and Jorick came to her side. "This must be where the gnolls were headed."

Evin looked over the ruins skeptically. "Where?"

he asked. "All I see are broken buildings and vines. There's nothing here."

Betilivatis sighed. "The trail doesn't lie," she said. "We're here."

"Well, then, Bet," Jorick said. "Maybe you should check your spell and make sure you did it right." Waving his hand toward the ruins, he stomped his foot. "Do you see any gnolls? Any villagers?"

Betilivatis crossed her arms. "I did it right."

She and Jorick continued to bicker, but Evin ignored them.

Something deep within the ruins had caught his eye.

He wound past fallen stone homes until his two companions were out of sight, their voices faded.

Mud squelched beneath his boots as he reached the edge of the riverbank. He crouched behind an ornate column that had fallen across the rapids, turning the column into a makeshift bridge.

The setting sun cast deep shadows through the ruins. Evin tuned out the sounds of the river and focused his eyes forward.

Something was moving by a headless statue. Something large and not human.

The creature stopped for a moment as if to study the statue. Then it resumed moving—slithering almost—through the ruins. Evin watched as the thing rounded a pile of stone blocks and came out of the shadow cast by a nearby wall.

Evin took in a sharp breath. The creature was tall, maybe five times as tall as Evin, and immensely fat. Its body looked like a blue-gray maggot, only blown up to about a million times the size.

The monster held itself like a snake ready to strike. Its head was wide and fat, with a big gash of a mouth filled with sharp yellow teeth. Two crimson eyes darted back and forth between the destroyed buildings, as though searching for something. Two pairs of hands attached to two pairs of stubby, muscular arms reached out, grasping at the air.

This creature was bigger than anything Evin had ever seen, and his insides seized with fear. He took a step back as quietly as he could from the river and the fallen column.

Evin's foot hit a loose stone. The stone clattered away.

The monster's eyes stopped searching. Instead, they looked in the direction where Evin stood. And then, the monster began to head straight at him.

Chapter Nine

Evin crept backward, still in a crouch, keeping his eyes on the bulbous creature. It was definitely heading in his direction, but it was taking its time, stopping every now and again to lean over, pick up a piece of stone, and peer beneath it. The creature's body would swell momentarily before shrinking back to its normal size after examining each stone—as though it took in an annoyed breath—and then it would continue moving.

Evin reached a slanted piece of granite roofing. He darted behind it and pressed his back to the cool stone. Jorick and Betilivatis were close by, standing in the tall grass beyond the southern border of the ruins and still fighting.

"I don't care about your stupid blue trail." Jorick said. "I know what I see."

"There must be an explanation." Betilivatis crouched and examined the ground. "And if you'd stop yelling for one moment, I could figure it out."

"Hey," Evin called out in as hushed a voice as he could manage. "Hey!"

They didn't hear him.

Evin found a smooth pebble. He tossed it and the small rock flew through the air. It hit Jorick's temple.

"Hey!" Jorick cried. Rubbing the side of his forehead, he looked over to where Evin was crouched. "What did you do that for?"

Evin put his finger to his lips and beckoned Jorick and Betilivatis over.

"What is it?" Jorick asked in an excited whisper as he set the food sack down near the base of the fallen roof. "Are the gnolls here? Did you find them?"

Evin shook his head. "No, no gnolls, but there's some creature moving around up there. I think it heard me while I spied on it, and now it's trying to find me."

Betilivatis raised her eyebrows. "A creature? Some sort of monster?" Not waiting for Evin to respond, she stood and peered around the edge of the roof. Jorick didn't hesitate in joining her. Both looked over the darkening ruins for a moment. Then, as one, they slowly lowered themselves back behind the roof.

"Well," Betilivatis said, her voice strangely excited. "That is a thing to see. And it's getting close."

"Definitely." Jorick's face grew stern. In one quick

move, he unsheathed his sword and held it aloft with both arms, then looked to Evin. "Should I take it down before it gets us first?"

Evin shook his head. "We don't know what that thing is or what it's capable of. We can't just rush in and fight it."

"It's big, it has sharp teeth, it's looking for us, and it's standing between us and wherever the gnolls took our friends. I bet the gnolls put it here as a trap."

"We don't know that," Evin said. "We need to stay low and take a look in that book Betilivatis has." Evin gestured at her leather satchel. "Would Zendric have written about it?"

Betilivatis nodded, then began digging through her satchel. "Of course. In fact I think I recall seeing a painting in the *Practical Guide* that looks just like—"

"Do I hearing things?"

The words weren't spoken by Evin, Jorick, or Betilivatis. They stood still in near silence, the only sounds being that of their breathing.

"I do hear things. I knowing I do. Somethings are nearing to me."

The voice was close, coming from the other side of the roof. It sounded as if the speaker were talking through a vat of goo, the words all thick and phlegmy.

Stones crunched and grass rustled as the large beast moved across the ground on the other side of the fallen roof, coming closer. Evin's chest seized in fear and—strangely—excitement.

Again he put his finger to his lips, then gestured with his head for both Jorick and Betilivatis to follow him. All three pressed their backs against the stone roof, and as quietly as they could, sidled in the opposite direction of the creature's voice.

They reached the edge of the roof just as the shadow of the monster's giant head came into view. Then they rushed around the edge and flattened themselves against a wall covered with fading carvings.

Evin peered around the edge of the wall toward the roof. Betilivatis did the same.

The creature was there, so terrifyingly close, and seemed even bigger than before. It ran the pudgy fingers of its two left hands against the fallen roof as muscles in its lower body tensed and relaxed, moving the monster's bulging body forward. Its twin red eyes, set on either side of its face like a fish's, darted back and forth.

It hadn't seen them.

Evin almost let out a sigh of relief—but then, he saw the food sack still lying where Jorick had left it.

The creature moved over the sack. Then it stopped

abruptly. Tilting its head, it bent over the entire top half of its bulging body and picked up the sack with two of its stubby arms.

The beast lifted the sack up to its face and sniffed. The dark liquid of the now crushed jars of preserves dripped down its belly. The creature sniffed once, twice, then tossed the sack aside.

It looked straight forward, directly at what little of Evin's face he'd dare show around the edge of the roof.

Evin pulled back. The sounds of the creature's movements became louder, quicker.

It called out in its phlegmy voice, "I seeing you! Come here!"

No one had to say anything. Evin, Jorick, and Betilivatis tiptoed past the carved wall and out into the open. Evin's eyes darted back and forth. He pointed at a fallen, cracked brass bell on the other side of the river.

The three kids clambered over the slippery, fallen column Evin had hidden behind earlier. Pieces of the column crumbled at their touch, falling and plunking into the surging water. But the river wasn't wide and they made it across quickly, then ran to dive behind the bell—just as the beast came past the wall. Evin peered again at the creature. It was coming right for them.

"Come on," he whispered to his friends, his tone urgent.

"Stay low to the ground and try not to make any noise."

Crawling on his hands and knees, Evin scurried over the broken cobblestone street to their next hiding place. Rock bit into his palms and scraped his knees, but he didn't care. All he could focus on was what he did best: hide. Behind him, he heard a great splash as the beast waded through the water.

Remnants of an old gazebo in what must have once been a park proved perfect cover, the park having long since been overgrown by tall weeds. Evin dived behind the gazebo just as the loud sound of the bell crashing against the ground rang out into the dusk. The monster must have tossed it aside.

Again Evin peered out from his hiding spot. Again he saw the beast. This time, it was farther away. Even though it was mostly in shadow in the fading light, the way it moved around in circles gave Evin the impression that it was confused.

Lowering himself down to sit behind the crumbling gazebo, Evin let out a shaky breath, then a small laugh. Looking at his companions, he grinned.

"See, stealth is the way to go. I think we lost it."

Jorick shrugged, his hands clenching the hilt of his sword tight. "I'd feel safer if it wasn't still moving around trying to find us," he whispered.

Evin looked past Jorick at Betilivatis. "We need to look in—"

"Way ahead of you," she said. Zendric's *A Practical Guide to Monsters* lay open in her lap and she flipped through its yellowing pages so fast that Evin wasn't sure how she could possibly be able to read anything. It was already getting hard to see with the sun going down.

"Ah ha, here," she said. "Looks like our monster is called an ormyrr." Smoothing the pages down, Betilivatis began to recite from Zendric's writing. " 'They aren't particularly aggressive, tending to keep to themselves.' And looks like they prefer to eat river animals, not humans, usually."

"Tell that to this ormyrr," Jorick muttered.

"Tell us what else it says," Evin said. Leaning over Jorick, he looked down at the book to see a painting of the ormyrr. Grublike body, four arms, sharp teeth—it was definitely the same beast.

"Well," Betilivatis began.

The ground rumbled and the gazebo Evin sat against was uprooted and flew into the air.

Evin fell backward into dry dirt squirming with worms and pillbugs. Beside him, Jorick and Betilivatis fell backward as well.

All three looked up into the dimming sky as they heard a great crash in the distance as the gazebo landed somewhere in the ruins. The ormyrr towered above them, its red eyes glowing in the light from the setting sun.

The creature stood in silence for a moment, watching the three kids who lay frozen in terror.

Then, its lips pulled back to reveal its sharp, yellow teeth.

Chapter Ten

These are the things, ay?" The ormyrr bent over and studied Evin's face. Drool dripped from its terrifying teeth, plopping like oversized raindrops in the dirt next to Evin's head. Evin held his breath, his heart thudding, certain that the creature was about to bite him in half. Instead, it moved to look at Jorick, then Betilivatis.

The ormyrr pulled back up to its full height and let out a booming sigh. "Boring. Nothing good with these things here. Gnollies took all good things."

Muttering about "stupid gnollies," the ormyrr then turned and headed back into the ruins, leaving the three unharmed.

Jorick leaped to his feet, his eyes on the retreating form of the beast. "Did you hear what it said?" he asked, his voice shrill. "About gnollies? It must mean the gnolls! It saw them!" Not waiting for Evin to recover—or even to ask him what to do—Jorick ran after the ormyrr, shouting, "Hey! You! Wait!"

"Your friend is ridiculously impulsive," Betilivatis said to Evin as she collected the fallen *Practical Guide* and her satchel.

Evin jumped up, scowling. "He never used to be," he said. He left Betilivatis behind and chased after the ormyrr as well.

Evin caught up to Jorick near the statue where Evin had first seen the ormyrr. The ormyrr had stopped and was now digging through what looked like a pile of pottery shards.

Jorick held his sword in both arms, his biceps bulging from the weapon's weight. Though hunched over, the ormyrr still towered over Jorick.

"Ormyrr!" Jorick shouted. "You've seen the gnolls come through here! I demand you tell me where they went or . . . or I'll run you through!" He brandished his sword menacingly.

Evin held his breath. The ormyrr stopped picking through the pottery shards and slowly rotated its head in Jorick's direction. The beast's red eyes looked the small human boy up and down.

Then, the ormyrr turned back to its menial task.

Jorick raised the sword high. "Hey, did you hear me?" he screamed. "I'm telling you to tell me where the gnolls went or I'll hurt you!"

The ormyrr ignored him.

"Jorick," Evin hissed. "The book said it's not aggressive, but this thing can toss small buildings like they're nothing. Don't make it mad."

"But it has to tell us where the gnolls took my dad!" Jorick said. He looked up at Evin, his eyes shimmering with tears. "It has to!"

The ormyrr's two top arms ceased digging and instead reached up to stick two fingers into two small holes that must have been the creature's ears. The ormyrr began to hum to itself.

Evin tried to pull Jorick back. "We need to talk to it nicer if we want its help," he whispered. "Attacking everything isn't always the way to go, you know."

"Talk!" Jorick shoved his sword through his belt then flung his hands in the air. "Why do you always want to talk? It's a monster! Can't you just throw your knives at it and make it talk?"

Evin clenched his fists. "What is wrong with you lately? Just calm down and I'll—"

At that moment, a massive ball of phlegm landed in the dirt at their feet, bits of spittle splashing onto their boots. Reflexively, both Evin and Jorick jumped back.

Evin looked up. The ormyrr towered above them, its teeth bared. It cleared its throat, then hawked another giant loogie to the ground.

"I is searching!" it boomed. "I will make you meal iffing you not shut it! Unless . . ." It rubbed its many hands together. "Do you be seeing things? Nice things?"

Jorick scowled. "What? What things?"

"Things!" the ormyrr said. "I be searching for so longs for things. Gnollies had interesting things, many of them, gears and magic and oh! Such wondrous things!"

Darting forward, the creature leaned over its bulbous body and looked Jorick in the eye. Its massive face was as wide as Jorick was tall. "Be giving things, I be helping find gnollies, yes?"

Evin took a tentative step back. The ormyrr's hot breath washed over his face. It smelled of fish left to sit out in the sun for three days, and his stomach roiled.

"We have no idea what you're talking about," Evin said. His voice was confident, but he couldn't keep his hand from trembling. "We don't have any . . . things. All we had was in our food sack and you crushed it."

"Wells," the ormyrr said, turning its gaze to Evin. "Then I needs to open up you and see if anything interesting inside you."

The ormyrr's froglike lips pulled back farther and farther, revealing its rows of razor-sharp teeth. All four of its pudgy hands clenched into fists. Slowly the ormyrr's terrifying, shredding mouth opened wide.

"W-wait!" Evin cried as he grabbed Jorick's arm and began to pull him away. "Wait, we—"

Hundreds of bright white sparks flashed above Evin's head, right in front of the ormyrr's face. The flashes were mesmerizing, like dozens and dozens of fireflies flitting around in a summer evening.

"Oh," the ormyrr said, ceasing to move. "Ohhhhh is BOOTIFUL! So WONDERING!" Rearing back to its full height, the creature reached out with its arms. As its hands shoved amid the fluttering circle of sparks, the image rippled like a reflection in a pond and the sparks disappeared.

Evin blinked at the sudden absence of light. In the time they'd taken to run from and then run to the ormyrr, it was now almost fully night. But the ormyrr didn't hesitate. It rushed forward toward something it saw behind Evin and Jorick. Both boys dived out of the way just in time to avoid being crushed by the creature's massive body.

From where he landed amid the rubble, Evin looked back and saw the ormyrr come to a halt directly in front of the slender figure of Betilivatis. She stood there, her white robes and copper hair swirling around her. A glowing ball of orange light hovered in front of her chest. In one outstretched hand she held open *A Practical Guide to Monsters*, the other held the carved wand. On her face she wore a smirk.

"You!" The ormyrr looked the elf girl up and down with wonder in its blood red eyes. "You is magic doing!"

Betilivatis nodded. "That I am."

The ormyrr leaned forward quickly, and for a moment Evin thought that it would eat her whole. Instead, it spread its bulbous body over the ground at Betilivatis's feet.

It was bowing.

"I must sees more!" it shouted, its thick voice partially muffled by the dirt. "Please giving me more!"

Dazed and surprised, Evin got to his feet and walked around the giant, grubby body of the ormyrr to stand at Betilivatis's side. Jorick followed.

"What did you do?" Evin whispered in Betilivatis's ear.

Betilivatis merely smiled wider, then held the *Practical Guide* up higher so that Evin and Jorick could read it.

" 'While (or perhaps because) these creatures have no talent for casting spells,' " Evin read aloud, " 'they find magic absolutely irresistible. They will lie, cheat, and steal to obtain a scroll, spellbook, or other magical object, and can be mesmerized by a skillful display of magic powers.' "

"Pleeeeeease!" the ormyrr begged. "I giving anythings you want!" Lifting its head up from the dirt, the ormyrr looked at Betilivatis with pleading eyes. "I is riched. Much very so! I giving golds! Lots of golds!"

Evin crossed his arms and looked down at the pitiful monster. "According to this book, you're probably lying," he said.

The ormyrr shuffled across the ground and reared back so that it could grasp Betilivatis's robes with two hands. She didn't flinch.

"No!" it whined. "Truths is all I giving! So many gold coins, they all yours, promisings! Just give me magic!"

With a prim cough, Betilivatis closed *A Practical Guide to Monsters* and shoved it back in her satchel. "Tell you what," she said to the ormyrr. "I'll make you a deal."

"Anythings!" the ormyrr said.

"All right. Tell me where the gnolls that came through here went, and I'll give you something magical so that you don't have to dig through these ruins anymore in search for mystic artifacts. Afterward, you will leave this place and leave us alone."

The ormyrr let go of Betilivatis's robes and reared up to its full height, its teeth bared into what Evin hoped was a smile. "It is a dealing!"

Evin, Jorick, Betilivatis, and the ormyrr all waited expectantly, looking among one another.

"Well?" Jorick finally said. "Where did they go?"

The ormyrr cleared its throat again. "Magic things first."

Sighing, Betilivatis stepped forward. Whispering words of magic, she held her wand aloft and twirled it in a circle above the palm of her other hand. Tendrils of pink and green smoke wove over her fingers before swirling together in her palm to form a crystal orb. Inside the orb, more of the white sparks danced.

Taking in a sharp breath, the ormyrr reached forward to snag the orb from Betilivatis's hands. Betilivatis clutched the orb tight and stepped back.

"Ah ah," she scolded. "The location of the gnolls?"

"Yessings, of courses," the ormyrr said while nodding its massive head repeatedly. "The gnollies took their two-legged things down."

"Down?" Evin asked.

The ormyrr nodded again. "Yesses, down. Under ruinings. There."

The creature extended the pointer fingers of its left hands to indicate something behind the trio. Evin turned to follow its gesture and saw a round copestone in the ground that looked to be about five feet in diameter. Atop the stone were faded etchings that Evin couldn't read.

"Ah ha," Betilivatis said, almost to herself. "So that's why my trail stopped here. They are here, just beneath us." She smirked at Jorick. "Told you."

Jorick just scowled.

The ormyrr cleared its throat, and Betilivatis turned back to it. "Thanks, big fellow," she said. She tossed the shimmering, magical orb in the monster's direction. "As promised."

Clapping its two lower hands in childlike glee, the ormyrr caught the orb in its upper hands and promptly fell onto its back. With the flickering magical light reflecting in its red eyes, the ormyrr placed the orb in what passed for a lap on its sluglike body and stared at the object, mesmerized.

Betilivatis looked between Jorick and Evin, then turned to head toward the copestone. "Looks like it's a good thing I came," she said over her shoulder. "Where would you boys be without me?"

Evin ran to her side. "I was handling the ormyrr," he said in a low voice. "But, I suppose, thanks for your assistance."

"Assistance?" Bet let out a prim laugh and stormed ahcad.

A strong hand slapped Evin's back and he looked over to see Jorick grinning at him. "Maybe you were right," he said. "Sometimes magic can come in handy."

Evin glared at Betilivatis's shadowy form, then shook his head. "Yeah," he said. "I was right."

Chapter Eleven

Thimself.

"This was definitely moved recently."

Evin stood up and brushed the dirt off his knees. Moments before, he'd crawled around the lip of the copestone while Betilivatis held aloft her magical light so he could see.

"How do you know?" Jorick asked, crouching down to look for himself.

"It's hard to make out," Evin told him, "but there are scratches in the ground from when this was moved. If the scratches were old, they'd be eroded by rain and wind. These are definitely fresh." He grinned, then looked over at Betilivatis. "Just a trick my brother taught me so you can know if anyone's gone through a door recently before you sneak in."

Betilivatis raised an eyebrow.

"Help me shove it open," Evin said to Jorick as he bent down to push. Jorick nodded and joined him.

Crouched together side by side, Evin and Jorick leveraged their feet against the dusty ground of the ruins and shoved against the wide copestone. The stony edge bit into Evin's palm. His back, leg, and arm muscles ached with the effort, but the round stone moved only a few inches. There was a loud screech as it moved over the old, cracked street.

Evin and Jorick leaned back, panting. "Care to help?" Evin asked Betilivatis.

"No, I'm good," she said.

Jorick rolled his eyes and both boys crouched back down and pushed again.

With three more shoves, the copestone suddenly seemed to open of its own accord, screeching across the ground to reveal a gaping hole. An old set of stone stairs disappeared beneath the long destroyed city.

Jorick stood to his full height and wiped the sweat off his forehead. "Now what?"

"Now we see if that ormyrr was telling the truth," Evin said. He turned to Betilivatis. "Bring the light—"

But the girl was running off into the darkened ruins. She had left her glowing orb behind to light the boys' efforts, having cast a second one for herself.

"Where are you going?" Evin called after her. "Bet!"

"My name is not . . . oh, never mind!" Her voice echoed among the crumbling buildings. She looked back over her shoulder. "I'm making sure the ormyrr actually left. We don't want it following us, begging for more magic and drawing the gnolls' attention. Be right back!"

And then Betilivatis—or Bet now, Evin thought, since she seemed through arguing about her name—was gone, her shadowy form and her little glowing light disappearing behind ancient walls.

"We don't really have time for this," Jorick grumbled as he came up behind Evin. "That ormyrr wouldn't be able to fit down those stairs anyway."

Evin clenched his fists, eyes not leaving the darkened ruins where Bet had disappeared. Her attitude was starting to get on his nerves, and Jorick was right: their families were down there, waiting. It had been a whole day already since the gnolls had kidnapped the villagers, and with every passing minute it became more and more likely that their relatives were being served up as a gnoll feast.

Turning back toward the dark stairway that led underground, Evin pushed past Jorick. "You're right, we don't have time for this. We're leaving her behind."

Evin reached the edge of the stairwell before he realized Jorick hadn't followed. He spun on his heels. "Well?" he asked. "Come on."

"But you said we needed her for the book and her magic," Jorick said.

"Well, I changed my mind," Evin said. "And you don't like her anyway. Don't you want to save your dad?"

"But the book. . . ."

Though Evin hated to admit it, Jorick was right: they needed Bet. Evin took in a few deep breaths and let himself calm down.

"All right," he said after a moment. "Yeah, sorry. Stay here and guard the stairs. I'm going after Bet."

Evin headed east into the ruins. He passed the shattered remains of the old stone gazebo and the brass bell as he walked, then rounded several walls and a few pillars. It was so dark now, and he could barely see his way around the destroyed buildings. He strained his eyes and tried to focus on his other senses like Marten had taught him—rogues often had to sneak through dark places, after all—but that didn't make it any easier.

The night was eerily quiet, save for the distant sound of the river's rushing water. Then, as he ducked underneath an arch, Evin heard Bet's voice coming from up ahead.

"I told you," she said in a hushed whisper. "The ormyrr wasn't going to be any threat anyway, so I took care of it myself so we could move on."

Evin stopped, unsure of what he'd just heard. He strained to listen.

For a long moment, Bet didn't say anything. Then Evin heard her sigh. "I understand. Yes, we're well on our way. I promise this will cease to be boring very soon."

It sounded as though she was talking to someone. He snuck forward and crouched behind a row of scrubby bushes that had managed to grow between the old stone roads. Peering between the branches, he saw Bet sitting cross-legged in a group of wildflowers with her back to him. Her conjured ball of light hovered in front of her.

Evin strained his eyes, but he could see no one else. There was another long stretch of silence.

"All right." Bet stood and brushed off the back of her robes. Her satchel lay open on the ground, and a book—one larger and thicker than *A Practical Guide to Monsters*—lay open among the flowers.

She gathered up the book and the satchel, then headed back toward the copestone. The ball of light followed behind her like a faithful puppy.

Evin lowered himself to hide in the shadows of the bushes as she came near. Bet didn't notice him. Staying low to the ground, he watched her ankles as she wove past all of the fallen arches he'd struggled not to stumble over on his trek to find her.

And then, the glow of her magic light faded and Bet was gone.

Evin stayed in his hiding spot, watching the spot where Bet had been talking, sure that he might see some hidden figure emerge. But no one was there.

What had he just seen? Evin wondered. Could she have been talking to herself? Reciting into some sort of magical diary that recorded her spoken words? Whatever it was, Evin's heart began to thud as he realized Jorick's first impression of Bet had been right—there was something decidedly creepy about the girl.

For a long moment, Evin crouched there, unsure what to do. Then slowly, he got to his feet and ran as quickly as he could back through the ruins.

When he neared the copestone and the subterranean stairs, he saw Bet and Jorick chatting. Her twin glowing orbs had merged together into one and the light was brighter, painting the ruins in sunny orange.

Evin stopped at the edge of light. A heavy unease coursed through him. Bet was smiling, but the expression seemed strange on her, strained.

He wanted to march up to her, jab his finger in her chest, and demand she tell him what she was doing in the ruins, who she'd been talking to, because clearly she'd lied about checking on the ormyrr. He sucked in a breath, straightened his shoulders, and marched through the grass toward his two companions.

Before Evin could say anything, Jorick caught sight of him. "You're back! Now can we go?"

Bet turned to face him, her eyes scanning him up and down. Evin clenched his fists, prepared to shout accusations—and then he saw the *Practical Guide* clutched in her hands.

His eyes darted from the book to the dark, underground stairwell, then back to the book. The gnolls were down there—a lot of them—as well as who knew what else. If Evin sent Bet away, he and Jorick would not only be going in literally blind without her magic light, they would be completely unprepared for whatever it is they should face.

Marten was down there. His parents. He needed to rescue them. And so, even though looking at Bet made him tremble with feelings of betrayal, he couldn't send her away. Not yet, anyway.

"Why are you just standing there? Are you ready to lead the way?" She put a hand on her hip. "I assume you want to go in first."

Evin took in a deep breath. "Actually," he said, "I want Jorick to go first, then you, and I'll take up the rear."

"Really?" Jorick asked. "Why?"

"Because you've got the biggest sword." Evin patted his friend on the shoulder. "A gnoll will think twice about messing with us when it sees that! Now, let's get going."

Gesturing toward the stairwell, Evin smiled. Bet's magical light obediently floated up to rest in front of her chest and light their path. As soon as Bet passed in front of him, Evin dropped the fake smile, his eyes not leaving the back of her head as he took his first step down the crude stone stairs leading down into the gnolls' lair.

Chapter Twelve

The farther down they went the colder it became, and the heavier the darkness seemed even with Bet's magic light. Evin's arms shivered and prickled with goose bumps. Calcified stalactites hung from the edge of the sloping, stone ceiling. Evin felt quite certain that at any moment one might snap off and impale them.

"So, Bet," Jorick whispered as they continued their seemingly endless descent. "What other magic can you do?"

"I thought you didn't trust magic," Bet whispered back.

"Well . . . what you did with the ormyrr was sort of impressive." Evin saw Jorick's shoulders rise and fall. "I was just wondering: can you make all the gnolls explode or something? That would make this much easier."

Bet let out a small laugh. "I'm afraid not. I'm still learning magic. There are limits to what I can do."

"What's that?" Evin asked. "You admit you're not all-powerful?"

"Hey," Jorick whispered, craning his head back to look at Evin. "It's not like we're—"

"Watch out!" Bet cried.

The crash happened so fast that Evin wasn't sure what happened. All he heard was a grinding of stone against stone, then a flash of white robes as Bet leaped forward and barreled into Jorick. An instant later, the roof crumbled right in front of Evin, so close he felt the craggy stone brush against his nose. Sharp stalactites clanged against the stairs. Dust rose in little clouds.

Bet's light snuffed out. Evin scrabbled backward up the stairs, coughing. It took a moment for realization to set in: Jorick had sprung a trap. He and Bet could be crushed beneath stone, impaled by stalactites. "Jorick!" Evin called. "Jorick!"

"Evin!" Jorick called back.

"Shh!" Bet hissed from the darkness. "We're all right. Stay quiet."

Evin opened his mouth to protest, but she was right—who knew how close to the gnolls' lair they were. The din of the trap crashing down could have alerted the gnolls to the arrival of intruders and sent the beasts running.

Evin strained his ears, expecting at any moment to hear the distant sound of claws against stone, the mocking howling of the vicious gnolls. His heart thudded.

After a long moment, Evin finally let loose the breath he hadn't realized he'd been holding. No gnolls were coming.

"Light your orb," Evin whispered into the darkness.

Bet didn't say anything, but Evin heard her muttering, and a moment later, an orange glow pierced the darkness.

In front of Evin, blocking the way down the stairs, lay the sprung trap. He saw it clearly now: The thick, heavy stone slab that had fallen was perfectly square, obviously not naturally formed. Peering beneath it, Evin realized that the stalactites weren't stalactites at all—they were metal spikes painted white. Through the forest of spikes, he could make out Jorick's boots and the white hem of Bet's robes.

"Climb over," Bet said.

"I was going to," Evin whispered back.

The slab was slanted on the stairs, and he scooted down it carefully. He landed on a step next to Jorick and brushed his hands to remove the dust. He glanced back at the trap and a hollowness filled him. Jorick had been so close to dying. If it hadn't been for Bet, Jorick would have been impaled by the trap—a trap Evin would have seen if he hadn't been so busy worrying about Bet's strange behavior.

"Thanks," Jorick whispered to Bet. He smiled.

"Not a problem," Bet said, smiling back. "Want to lead the way?"

"I will," Evin interjected. "I'm going first in case there are any more traps."

"Why?" Bet asked. "So you can spring them?"

"No, so I can disarm them."

Jorick and Bet gave each other a look, but didn't argue. Evin stormed ahead down the stairs. He scanned the walls, straining to see any signs of traps so he could prove that he, too, knew how to handle them.

After an achingly long time, Evin finally saw the glow of torchlight.

Ahead was an open square doorway beyond which lay a large, empty room.

Evin started to move forward, then stopped, grinning. "Hold on." He raised a hand to halt his companions. "There's another trap here."

Jorick and Bet stayed back as Evin followed the wire with his eyes. Midway up the wall on his right, the wire was attached to a hook that jutted from the stone. It ran across the center of the doorway, at a height that would make it hard for anyone over five feet to walk over or under unless they had exceptionally long legs. The wire was threaded through an eye hook in the left wall. From there the wire ran up to the ceiling and was connected to . . .

"There," Evin whispered.

Above them was another false ceiling equipped with several dozen razor-sharp spikes painted white.

"Can you disarm it?" Jorick whispered.

"I may have a spell—" Bet began.

Evin shushed her and leaned forward, studying the trap's system. With his left hand, he clutched the wire tight, holding it taut. With his right, he unhooked the wire from the wall.

He stood, holding the trip wire in both hands, his arms straining with the effort. If he let the wire slacken even a little, the roof—and its deadly spikes—would come crashing down upon him. Not giving the wire even an inch of release, he stood on his tiptoes and studied the left wall, searching until he found what he was looking for.

A barely visible second hook jutted out about two feet up the wall above the eye hook. Evin looped the wire over the top hook, then down through the eye hook, and back up again. He grinned as he realized this was exactly the way the gnolls must have done it. Then he attached the end of the wire to the top hook.

For a moment, Evin stood there holding the wire, afraid to let go. He held his breath and looked up. The spikes trembled, just barely, and for a moment Evin feared they'd come tumbling down upon him.

Still not breathing, Evin slowly pulled first one hand and then another away. The trip wire stayed as taut as it had been when stretched across the entryway, and the ceiling stayed in place.

Evin finally breathed.

Turning to his friend and Bet, he smiled. "All that practice with Marten paid off."

Jorick returned Evin's grin and slapped his back. "Good job," he whispered.

"See?" Evin said to Bet. "Magic is definitely handy, but it's not always necessary."

Bet raised both eyebrows. "I suppose so. Shall we continue on?"

Evin nodded and once more led the way. Quietly, gingerly, the trio stepped through the opening at the base of the stairs into the diamond-shaped room beyond.

Evin, Jorick, and Bet all looked around in silence. Tall wooden doors lined the angled walls and at the opposite end, the room narrowed into a hallway.

"There's no one here," Jorick said.

"We can see that," Bet whispered.

Ignoring her snide tone, Jorick looked up at the high, stony ceiling. "Maybe the ormyrr was lying after all. Maybe this is just some long abandoned storehouse and there's nothing here."

"No, there's something here—or at least there was." Evin pointed to the floor. It was covered with muddy tracks made by hundreds of pawlike feet, creating a strange mottled pattern. "The copestone was moved recently, remember? And I know that trap was new. Also, the torches are lit."

"Then maybe you two can keep it down before we attract attention," Bet hissed. She adjusted the strap of her satchel and strode forward, her footsteps barely making any sound.

The room seemed so open and exposed that Evin's chest felt tighter than the trip wire. There were no shadows here in which to skulk. Nothing to hide behind should something round the corner. He quickened his step.

They were almost to the hallway when Evin heard a door creak.

He spun around. One of the doorways near the stairway's entrance had opened. A low, terrifying noise echoed in the diamond-shaped chamber. It was the same staccato, howling laughter Evin had heard the night he watched Hesiod go down in flames.

As he watched, frozen in place, a gnoll stepped out of the doorway.

The monster was tall—seven feet at least—and wore a piece of metal over its chest that appeared to have been pounded over and over with a rock. The gnoll stood on what looked like the hind legs of a dog, its shaggy, orange tail wagging slowly behind it. A panting tongue lolled out of its low-slung head. Drool dripped from its sharp teeth.

Brandishing a stained battle-axe as long as the creature was tall, the gnoll took a step forward, its sharp canine nails clacking against the stone floor. Its mocking, laughing howl grew louder and higher in pitch.

Before Evin, Jorick, or Bet could react, there came the sound of another high-pitched disturbing howl from directly behind them.

They had nowhere to run.

Chapter Thirteen

Evin pulled his daggers free and held them ready.

This was it. His first real fight. He'd practiced for so long. He had to be ready. He just had to.

"Stand back to back to back so that we all face out," Evin commanded, willing the shakiness out of his voice.

Jorick turned toward the gnoll that had emerged near the narrow hallway. The creature listened to their frightened breaths with only one ear. The other appeared to have been bitten off. Evin and Bet stared down the orange-furred gnoll that had emerged near the stairway.

"Draw your weapons," Evin said, his tone steady. "This is exactly what we've been practicing for all these years, right, Jorick?"

The gnolls both took a step forward. The orange gnoll pulled back its lips to reveal black gums and sharp teeth.

"You really think we can do this?" Jorick asked.

"We have to," Evin said over his shoulder. "Just think of your dad. If we don't beat these things, he loses too."

Jorick grunted. "All right. All right."

"You ready, Bet?" Evin asked.

Bet let out an annoyed sigh. "Of course. This is nothing." She slipped her wand out of the folds of her robe.

Sharp toenails clacked against the muddy floor as the gnolls took another step forward.

"Well, just in case, I'll help you with the orange one. Jorick, you go after the other one." Evin took in a deep breath. "Go!"

Evin felt a rush of wind at his back as Jorick broke free and raced toward the one-eared gnoll. "Aaaargh!" the boy called out, a makeshift war cry.

"*Seero sueee eyeex!*" Bet cried at the same time, swirling her wand in a circle at a torch.

The torch's flame whooshed upward as though Bet had doused it with oil. Just as the orange-furred gnoll reared its head back to let out another high-pitched laugh, she sliced her wand through the air, pointing from the torch to the gnoll. The flames followed her wand, flying from the torch and engulfing the gnoll.

The gnoll's laugh turned into a scream as its body lit with fire. It dropped its battle-axe and fell to the floor, rolling to put out the flames. Its tail slapped against the floor in agony.

"Thanks for your help," Bet said, grinning.

Evin rolled his eyes and looked back at Jorick. The one-eared gnoll slashed down with its unwieldy axe while cackling in its strange, pulsing cry. Jorick met each of the monster's thrusts with his sword, parrying each blow as though he'd been doing it all his life. With each successful block, their blades clanged.

Jorick shouted and ducked the next blow. The one-eared gnoll lost its balance. The boy rolled out of the way as the gnoll stumbled forward, almost slipping on the muddy floor. Behind the gnoll now, Jorick cried out once more and cleaved down with his sword. The creature's tail fell to the floor and the gnoll howled.

"Evin!"

Evin spun to find that the scorched gnoll had managed to put the flames out and was advancing on Bet, its orange fur now burned black. The girl frantically dug around inside her satchel for spell components.

"Don't shout orders and then just stand there!" Meeting Evin's eyes, she gestured at the gnoll. "Distract it already!"

Evin's nostrils flared, but he nodded. He raced toward the singed gnoll, took a bracing breath, and leaped onto its back.

The beast growled and wrenched back and forth. Evin wrapped his legs around the monster's middle. The metal edges of its breastplate bit into the undersides of his knees. His arm clung around the gnoll's neck, choking it. With his free hand, Evin tried to stab the gnoll with one of his daggers, but the monster moved too quickly and he was unable to do more than make shallow cuts.

Bet pulled a vial of black liquid from her pack. Muttering words of magic, she uncapped the vial and flung the liquid in the singed gnoll's direction. She waved her wand at the resulting splatter and a black puddle appeared beneath the gnoll's feet. The creature slipped, stumbling forward onto its face and sending Evin flying to the ground.

He lay on his back, the wind knocked out of him.

"Sorry," Bet said halfheartedly.

He had no time to respond for at that moment the singed gnoll loomed over him, battle-axe raised high. With a howling laugh, it brought the blade down.

Evin rolled out of the way just as the axe hit the stone. Sparks flew. He leaped to his feet and watched every twitch of the monster's muscles.

The gnoll stared back at Evin, the monster breathing heavily.

Evin took a quick glance over his shoulder and saw Bet standing near the stairway entrance. And then he got an idea.

"Bet! Get this one to follow you up the stairs and then get clear!"

"No!" she cried back. "You take it toward the back wall and I'll—"

"Just do it!"

The gnoll attacked. The deadly edge of the battle-axe whizzed toward Evin's face and he dodged to his right. He felt the rush of the stained steel blade as it nearly sliced off his arm.

The gnoll didn't hesitate. It swung its axe again, and this time Evin ducked. Again the gnoll sliced, again he barely managed to dodge what was surely meant as a killing blow.

"Any time now!" he called out.

The singed gnoll raised its axe high and cackled. Evin took a breath, waiting . . . and then the gnoll brought the axe down. He flung himself down and forward, pulling himself into a ball and tumbling right between the gnoll's doglike legs.

He jumped up to his feet, temporarily back-to-back with his foe. Across the diamond-shaped room, he saw Jorick lash out with his sword as the one-eared gnoll attacked. The sword met the middle of the axe and split the wooden shaft in two as easily as though Jorick had sliced through a twig. The one-eared gnoll's arms flailed out, sending the two halves of the broken battle-axe flying across the room. The bladed half landed in the nearby wooden door with a *thunk* and stuck there.

The singed gnoll howled again. Evin spun around just in time to see his enemy swinging its battle-axe toward him. He gasped and tried to leap back, but he knew there was no time to dodge this blow. He was about to die.

But before the blade could hit him, the gnoll flew backward as though some invisible person had tackled it, taking the axe with it. It landed on its back and lay there, momentarily stunned.

At the entrance of the stairway, Bet stood with her wand held high, her lips twisting to form words of magic.

The singed gnoll leaped up to its feet, but Bet flicked her wand yet again. Hundreds of perfectly harmless, firefly-like sparks fluttered in front of the gnoll's face. The gnoll swatted at them then growled deep in its throat. Yipping in annoyance, it bounded toward Bet.

"Up the stairs!" Evin shouted at the wizard. "Hurry!"

Bet didn't hesitate. She spun around and raced up the stairs. "You better have a really good plan!"

Evin didn't respond. He held a dagger tightly in his right hand, watching and waiting.

The gnoll stepped over the door's threshold.

"Evin! Do something!" Bet's voice echoed from the stairwell. "It's coming!"

"Just a moment longer," Evin said calmly. He aimed the dagger like Marten taught him in target practice so many times.

The singed gnoll climbed the first of the steps.

"Now!" Evin whispered to himself. He let his blade fly.

There was a slicing sound as the dagger severed the taut trip wire, and a rumbling began as the false roof dislodged itself.

Confused, the gnoll looked up. It didn't even get a chance to scream before the faux stone roof crashed down on it, impaling the monster with dozens and dozens of razor-sharp spikes.

Black liquid squirted out from beneath the trap and splattered against the walls. Dust rose in little clouds.

Evin didn't give himself even a moment to celebrate. He turned to help Jorick only to find his friend panting as the one-eared gnoll lay in a heap on the muddy floor. The creature's eyes were rolled up into its head, its tongue lolled out of its snout, and it lay in a pool of black blood.

Jorick held his now stained sword high, his arms trembling. His eyes were wide as he stared at the monster he'd just finished off.

Slowly, Evin and Jorick met each other's gaze—and smiled.

"Whoa!" Bet called out.

Evin turned to see her stumbling over the top of the fallen trap. Jorick ran from across the room to help her. She took his hand and jumped down from the top of the trap.

"Good aim," Jorick said.

Evin grinned. "Lots of practice." He walked over to pick up his dagger.

"I can't believe it," Jorick said, hands on his hips, surveying the room. "We actually did it!"

Bet grabbed Jorick's arm. "Quiet down," she said in a hushed voice. "Listen."

"What?" Evin said. "I don't hear—"

"Shh!"

All three fell silent, straining their ears. Evin heard a distant *drop drop drop* of water falling into some unseen pool, and the crackling of the torches along the wall.

After a long moment, Bet let out a sigh of relief, then patted herself down as though making sure she was really all in one piece. "I was worried that all the commotion might cause other gnolls to come running," she whispered. "But these must have been the only two nearby."

"At least we know we're in the right place after all." Jorick's face broke out into a big grin. "Did you see me with that one-eared monster?" He cut his sword through the air. "The best part was when I ducked and then—"

"Quit it, Jorick." Evin brushed the sweat off his forehead. "There's a lot more of these monsters down here, and we barely managed to get past two." He pointed toward the narrow hallway at the other end of the room. "We don't have time for tales of glory. Our families are waiting. We need to move."

Chapter Fourteen

The hallway at the other end of the diamond-shaped chamber angled deeper underground. As they rounded a corner, Evin saw two openings on either side of the hall. He peeked through each passage. Aside from a few makeshift pieces of furniture, the rooms were empty.

As they walked, the dripping noise grew louder. The hallway ended with a giant pillar of natural stone that rose floor to ceiling. A narrow pathway curved around either side of the column.

Evin pressed his back against the stone pillar and inched his way around. He felt sure he'd find the army of gnolls that had attacked Hesiod on the other side.

Instead, he found himself inside a vast, empty, dark cavern.

A rush of cool air met his face, and mud squished under his boots.

"What is this place?" Jorick whispered as he stepped out from behind Evin. He walked deeper into the cavern— and then leaped back.

"There's a huge puddle here!" Jorick shook his drenched boot. "The water went all the way to my ankle."

"It's a natural cave," Bet said. She leaned against the stone pillar, her expression thoughtful. "You know, the layout of this lair is sort of familiar. . . ."

Jorick ignored her. "There's got to be another tunnel here somewhere." He felt his way along the sloping cavern wall, doing his best to keep out of the dark water. Moonlight shone through holes in the cavernous ceiling, but the light was so scant that it did little more than highlight the ripples on the water.

Drip drip drip. The noise echoed off the wall.

"Hmm," Bet said.

Evin turned away from Jorick and saw that Bet had the *Practical Guide* open in her hands. She smiled.

"What is it?" Evin asked.

Bet looked up at him and smiled in her mysterious way. "Follow me."

She brushed past Evin, not seeming to care that the hem of her fancy robe was soaking up stagnant water.

For a moment, Evin considered taking the book from her and leading the way himself. The *drip drip drip* echoed in his ears and he kept seeing her knowing, enigmatic smirk in his head. They set Evin's teeth on edge.

"Coming?" Jorick called. He was already following Bet.

Evin let out a long breath, trying to let his suspicions go. This was the quest he'd fantasized about going on all his life. This was supposed to be fun, after all. A big, grand adventure that—

No, Evin told himself. Not fun. A rescue mission. Daring rescue missions weren't supposed to be fun!

"Argh," Evin muttered to himself. Maybe the long day was finally getting to him. Maybe it was just exhaustion. But suddenly everything started to seem more complicated than it should. Shaking his head, he splashed through the water.

Bet led them around the edge of the massive cavern, taking care not stumble over underwater outcroppings of stone. Then, on the left side of the cavern, they discovered the opening of a dark tunnel. They tiptoed into another small hallway. Evin could barely make out a few torches along the wall, but they weren't lit. In the distance, he could hear the rumbling of voices.

Swirling her wand in a circle, Bet conjured a sphere of light and moved deeper down the hallway. They reached an intersection and she took them right, then another intersection that took them left. The halls were all empty, all dark. Aside from the distant mutterings that didn't seem to get any closer, there was no noise except for their footsteps and breathing.

Finally, they reached a wooden door. Putting his finger to his lips, Evin pressed his ear against the polished wood. He could hear the crackling of a fire on the other side, but nothing else.

Slowly, he opened the door. It creaked and he stopped, held his breath, and waited.

No gnolls came running, so he opened the door the rest of the way. Jorick and Bet crowded at his back to see inside.

In the center of the room was what must have once been a long table, but two of the legs were missing and the table lay against the ground at an angle. A fireplace with a flickering flame revealed cobwebs in the corners of the room.

The distant muttering that Evin had been hearing seemed to be coming from behind a door on the other side of the room. They were louder now.

"I hear voices ahead," he whispered, turning to face Jorick and Bet. "Maybe we—"

Evin stopped. Bet was gone.

Jorick tilted his head and leaned against the broken table. " 'Maybe we' should what?"

"Where's Bet?" Evin asked. As he said it, his stomach felt heavy.

"What?" Jorick asked. "She's right—Hey!" He spun

around. The room was small. There was no place she could be hiding. "Did the gnolls get her? We have to go back and—"

Evin jumped forward and grabbed his friend's arm. "Listen," he said, "I don't think anything got her. I think she left us. I have to tell you something: You were right about Bet."

"What?" Jorick scowled. The firelight sent shadows into the creases on his forehead. "I was going to tell you that I was wrong. She fought so well back there, and without her I'd have been killed by that trap. She's not so bad."

Evin nodded. "She did fight well," he said. "Even if she did insist on arguing with me the whole time."

"Is that what this is about?" Jorick asked. "Are you mad that someone other than you is making decisions for once?"

"No," Evin said through gritted teeth. "No, it's not that. Back at the ruins, when I went to go find her, I saw—"

A panel beside the fireplace popped open. Evin leaped away from Jorick. Both boys pulled free the swords from their belts.

Bet walked through, smiling. Ignoring their swords, she rushed to grab their hands.

"I found them!" she said. "They're alive, and they're unguarded!"

"My dad?" Jorick said. His voice was full of joy, all thought of Bet's weird behavior suddenly gone. "You found my dad? Where?"

Bet pulled them around the fallen table toward the secret door she'd come through. "This way. There's a whole bunch of cages with people inside."

Evin pulled his hand free of Bet's. "Why didn't you tell us you were going to go find them?" he asked. "Why didn't you just take us with you?"

Bet adjusted the strap of her satchel and flipped her hair. "I said I'd be right back. Didn't you hear me? I was only gone for a moment. I just wanted to check something."

"Check what?" Evin asked.

Bet sighed, irritated. Opening up the *Practical Guide*, she turned to the center and showed Evin an intricate drawing of an underground lair. It was labeled "Typical Goblin Lair—Abandoned Gnome Burrowtown."

"Look," she said, pointing with her finger at the top left portion of the map. "See, this is the chamber we fought the gnolls in." Tracing a path with her finger, she continued on. "And this is the cavern we walked through, and these are the halls, and this is the room we're in now." Moving her finger to the top right portion of the map, she said, "And this is where I went."

She pointed at a section of the map in which several square boxes were labeled "Slave Pens."

"See, I knew this place was familiar." Bet pulled the book back and slammed it shut. "This must have been the goblin lair that Zendric based his drawing upon. I got the idea when I saw those old goblin paintings in the first chamber, and I just went to check my theory before we decided to run off down that other hallway." She gestured to the hallway behind Evin through which the muttering sounds came.

"Goblin lair?" Jorick asked. "Are the gnolls working for goblins, then?"

Bet shrugged. "Maybe that, or maybe they killed all the goblins and took over the place. It doesn't matter. All that matters is I found your villagers, and now we have a map of this place. What are you waiting for?"

Evin didn't know what to say. Part of him felt relieved. But the other part—the part that couldn't forget what he saw up above—couldn't bring himself to trust Bet.

They were so close. Marten, his parents, Jorick's dad, all the villagers—they were right down another hallway. After they saved them, Evin decided, then he'd confront Bet. What could she do against so many people? She'd have to hand over the *Practical Guide*.

Evin smiled. "Let's go," he said.

Chapter Fifteen

The hallway turned several corners and then reached another doorway. Tentatively, the trio peered through.

Moonlight spilled in through gaping holes in the ceiling. The room was carved from the earth and bisected by a stone-and-mortar wall that rose into the craggy cave ceiling and ended just before a giant, natural stone pillar at the south end of the room. To the left of the doorway, Evin could just make out stacks of wooden crates and barrels overflowing with baskets, pottery, and clothing. He thought he recognized Marten's dark coat in the pile.

And then he saw the cages.

From what Evin could tell in the low light, there were four of them on this side of the mortar wall. Each cage was as big as Hesiod's now destroyed town hall and packed with dozens and dozens of people.

"We did it, Evin!" Jorick whispered, his voice wavering. "We found them!"

The boy began to leap out from behind the doorway, but Evin and Bet each grabbed an arm to hold him back.

"We have to—" Evin whispered.

"We should—" Bet said at the same time.

Evin glared at Bet, and she glared back. He spoke again, still in a whisper. "We have to make sure there are no gnolls first. We're so close, we can't ruin it now."

Jorick swallowed and backed down. "All right."

The three studied the room. Evin listened for howls and the click of claws on stone. But all he heard was the soft crying of several of the captives. All he saw were the shadowy faces of people he vaguely recognized.

Bet looked at Evin, her eyebrow arched. He nodded. She waved her wand and conjured a small ball of light. Then, together they rounded the corner.

Mrs. Needman, the baker's wife, spotted the trio from the nearest cage. Her eyes widened and she began to shake. The old woman raised a hand to point at them. Her lips moved but no sound came out. Finally, she managed to say, "We're saved!"

And then all of the people in the cages turned to face the trio and began talking at the same time. Many rushed to the bars and shoved themselves against them, crying out, "Help us!" Evin saw other villagers he knew: Mr. and Mrs. Hammersmith and their daughter Nell, bulbous market overseer Manfred Wimple, and reedy stable boy Adam, whose last name Evin didn't know.

He did not, however, see his mother, father, or Marten. His heart sank, but he ran to the closest cage, reaching through grasping arms, searching for a lock.

"Evin, thank the gods you're here!" A woman's hand reached through the bars and grabbed his arm, and Evin looked up into the kind, tired eyes of Mary Wright, the mayor's wife. As she said his name, a rush of whispers began behind her in the cage before spreading to the pens nearby. The villagers were muttering, "It's Evin!" and "The innkeeper's son!" and "The boys have come to save us!"

Evin stopped fumbling for the lock. He felt so overcome by all these frightened, dirty people relying on him that he couldn't move.

Behind him came the echoing footsteps of Jorick and Bet. The cage grew brighter as Bet neared. Mary Wright and the other villagers shielded their eyes.

"Dad?" Jorick called. "Dad!" He stood in front of Mary Wright and clutched her hand. "Have you seen my father?" he asked.

Mary shook her head. "He's not in here, but he's in one of the cages. They put us all here and they're going to . . . oh gods. . . ."

"Don't worry," Evin said. "We'll get you out of here. All of you."

"Stop talking!" a voice cried out from the thick of the crowd behind Mary. "Those monsters will be back any moment!"

From beside Evin, Bet said, "I'm inclined to agree. You all are being far too noisy."

Inside the cage, Mary Wright blinked back tears and turned to the people behind her. "You heard the girl," she whispered. "Keep quiet." The whispering subsided, but Evin could almost feel everyone staring at him. All that trust and hope felt crushing. Adventure or no, this wasn't fun at all.

"I'm going to look in the next cage," Jorick said. Before Evin could tell him they should focus on one cage at a time, he disappeared into the hazy darkness.

Shaking his head, Evin resumed his search for the first cage's lock. He peered among the bars, doing his best to ignore the villagers who were watching him. Bet held her light up high. At last he spotted the lock on the north side of the cage, in the middle of the bars.

"Here!" Evin called, and Bet crept in closer.

"Are you sure you can get it?" she asked. "I could—"

"My brother showed me how to do this. It's easy." Evin pulled free his dagger and stuck the point in the keyhole. He twisted the blade side to side.

"Please," a small voice said from inside the cage. "They're going to eat us all."

Peering down, Evin saw little Kady Fairchild, his neighbor's daughter. The young girl watched him with wide, doll-like eyes that shimmered with impending tears, and memories bubbled into Evin's mind of the girl coming to the inn and having tea parties with Evin's mother when the tavern wasn't busy. Overcome by this simple memory, Evin's hands fumbled and he dropped his dagger. It clattered to the stone floor.

Bet sighed. "Move," she told Evin. "Let me try."

He didn't argue—he couldn't think enough to be angry. As he bent down to collect his dagger, all he could focus on were the orange-lit faces of the people packed together inside the cage. Memories of how they fit into his life swirled inside his brain, surging into his thoughts as though a floodgate had been opened.

Allen and Lam were there, brothers and tradesmen who spent many a night celebrating their good fortunes at the tavern, and who often slipped Evin sips of their ales when his mother wasn't looking.

Sera, a seamstress apprentice that Marten was sweet on, was here. She was one of the few people who could stop Evin's father from being all business long enough to sit down for a nice meal.

He saw Shon, the mayor's assistant whom he and Marten often practiced their pick pocketing upon, and who always got so satisfyingly huffy when he realized his handkerchiefs were missing.

All these people were a part of life in Hesiod, and yet for the past two days, all Evin focused on was saving his brother and his parents—when he wasn't busy focusing on how this was supposed to be a grand adventure or how annoying Bet was.

Why hadn't he thought of all these other innocent people earlier? Why hadn't he worked harder to save anyone when the village was burning? A rush of guilt washed over him.

With a clang, the cage's lock snapped open. Bet smiled down at Evin. "I think my way is easier." She slipped her wand back into her robes.

The bars around the lock glowed bright red, and inside the cage, the crowded villagers hugged one another. Evin grasped the bars of the cage and yanked back— but the door only opened a few inches before stopping with the jangle of chains. Startled, Evin looked at the cell door and saw that chains were attached to the top and bottom, allowing it to open only a small bit. Connected to the chains were two more padlocks.

"Of course," he muttered.

"What's wrong?" Evin heard Mary Wright ask. "Did you get it open?"

"Not yet," Evin said as loudly as he dared. "Bet, can you get the top lock? I'll get the bottom one and—"

"Evin!" Hearing Jorick's voice, Evin stopped and turned to see his friend race around the side of the cage.

"What is it?" Evin asked. "Did you find your father?"

"No, but I found Marten," Jorick said. "He's asking for you."

Evin stiffened as memories of the night Hesiod burned down rushed over him—memories of watching his brother get hit over the head with an axe.

"Bet, can you—" Evin started.

She waved a hand. "Go to your brother."

Evin looked back at Mary Wright. "You'll be free soon," he called.

The old woman smiled at him. "Thank you! So much!"

Bet's magic light faded behind them and the boys quickly plunged into relative darkness, the moonlight so scant that it was hard to make out what was in front of them. Jorick led Evin past the second and third cages, all the way to the last cage on that side of the cavernous room. There, pressed against the bars, was Marten. The boy slouched forward, his eyes unfocused, his blond hair mussed and tangled. As Evin ran to him, Marten looked up and muttered, "Evin. You must . . . help . . ."

"Don't worry," Evin said. "We're going to get you out of here." He felt for the first lock in the shadows. Finding it, he pulled out his dagger and jabbed it into the keyhole. This time his hands did not shake.

Other captured villagers surged around Marten, watching Evin work, but Evin ignored them. Worrying about the whole of the village was too much. He had to focus on one task at a time. As he strained with the lock, he spoke to his brother, the words spilling forth from his mouth unbidden.

"I'm so sorry I left you behind," he said. "But I was so scared. I—"

"It's all right," Marten wheezed. "Please, hurry."

Evin swallowed, then nodded. His knuckles straining, he gave the dagger one last twist—and the lock popped open.

"You did it!" Jorick cried, then pulled at the cage door. Just as before, the door opened only a few inches before stopping with a clang—the top and bottom chains were still in place. "You have got to be joking."

"It was the same at the first cage," Evin said, already crouching down to work on the lower lock. "But we can—"

From the other side of the cage came the sound of the gnolls' cackling howls.

Evin stiffened. One of Jorick's hands grabbed his shoulder, and the other reached for the sword at his side. For a moment, all of the villagers in the cages fell silent.

The howls grew louder, joined now by the clacking din of claws walking over stone. Evin peered around the side of the cage and saw torchlight beyond the stony pillar. Deep within the craggy southern tunnel, gnoll shadows loomed, coming closer and closer.

"Help us!" a fat woman said as she clutched the door right in front of Evin.

Marten was shoved against the bars and the door clanged, straining against its chains.

"We're all doomed!" a tall beanpole of a man said.

More of the villagers cried out, screaming in fear.

"Help," Marten gasped, his eyes bulging. "Help me out of here!"

"Hurry!" Jorick cried, tugging at Evin's arms. "Open the locks."

The staccato howls and the marching of many footsteps filled the room and Evin's heart began to pound. He needed to act fast, but he couldn't think, couldn't move.

Orange light enveloped Evin and Jorick as Bet ran past the other cages to their side. "We have to run!" she said.

"Did you get the other cage open?" Evin asked her. "Can you help me open this one?"

"There's no time!" Bet shouted. "We have to hide. There must be dozens of gnolls coming right this way." Grabbing Jorick's arm, she turned and ran away from the cages, dragging him toward the north side of the room, past the cages. He protested loudly, but she didn't lessen her grip.

Evin hesitated, his eyes darting from the growing shadows to the cages to Bet and Jorick. Finally his eyes came to rest on his brother, who had managed to slip his slender body halfway through the partially opened door.

"Help . . . me . . ." Marten wheezed.

Evin leaped to his brother's side and grabbed his free arm, then tugged as hard as he could. Behind Marten, several of the villagers shoved at his back. He grit his teeth. At last Evin fell to the ground from the force of his pulling. And Marten landed heavily on top of him.

"We have to . . . we have to run . . . ," Marten began.

Evin jumped up, then pulled his brother to his feet. He whispered to the villagers who were still trapped, "I'm sorry. We'll be back for you. We'll be back." Grasping his brother under his arms, Evin dragged Marten toward the crates and barrels at the north end of the room.

Mary Wright called out, "What about us? We're all going to die!"

He ignored her. He had to. There was no time to waste now.

Just as he and Marten dived behind a stack of barrels, torchlight flooded the walls. The howls of the gnolls rose above the wails of the villagers.

Dozens upon dozens of gnolls surged out of the hallway and into the room.

Chapter Sixteen

"Oh no oh no oh no," Marten said. He rocked back and forth next to Evin behind the barrels, his knees to his chest, his eyes blank. "They're back, oh gods they're back."

"Shhh," Evin whispered, placing a reassuring hand on his brother's shoulder. "They'll hear you. You're free now, don't worry. You're safe."

Marten ceased talking, but continued to rock. His eyes were glossy, unfocused.

"Help us!" he heard a woman scream. It sounded like Mary Wright, but Evin didn't want to think about what was about to happen to the woman now that he'd abandoned her.

The gnolls cackled, their chorus of howls echoing throughout the room. Rusty cage doors creaked open and Evin watched from among the barrels as the gnolls dragged the villagers out of the cages, shackled them, and forced them to walk toward the south end of the room where the square walls gave way to craggy stone tunnels.

Evin watched, helpless, as all of the villagers disappeared around natural stone pillars. Their cries and the gnolls' howling soon faded. The once crowded slave pens stood open and empty. From the scant moonlight, Evin saw that someone had dropped a rag doll on the stone floor, a button eye missing and its arm torn.

"They're all going to die," Marten muttered. "The monsters . . . they . . ."

Evin turned to his brother and studied the boy's face in what little light there was. Marten's eyes darted back and forth, looking at everything and nothing. His jaw had fallen slack, and his whole body shivered.

"We can save them," Evin whispered. "We can! They haven't eaten anyone yet, have they? There's no reason for them to start now. Bet, Jorick, and I are going after them. We'll find a way to rescue them. Don't worry."

Marten angled his eyes to look up at Evin through a shock of hair. "It won't work, Evin," he said, his voice scratchy. "We're all doomed."

This wasn't like Marten. Not at all. Marten always said that no matter how bad things could sometimes be, better times were just around the corner. Sometimes you had to work for those better times, but they were always there, waiting for you to find them.

Evin reached out a trembling hand and felt at the side

of Marten's head, where the gnoll's blade had hit him in Hesiod. He ran his fingers across Marten's scalp. The older boy's skin was cold to the touch, his hair stiff, brittle. And then Evin felt the dent hidden behind thick blond hair in the side of Marten's head.

Evin jerked his hand back. The dent wasn't deep, but could the blow have hurt Marten somehow? Permanently?

He didn't have time to think about it. Behind him came the shuffling of boots on stone, and bright orange light flared. Evin grabbed his daggers, prepared to attack, but instead found Jorick and Bet standing over him.

Bet cleared her throat. "Your brother, I presume?"

Evin looked up at her, squinting into the harsh light of her magic orb. "We managed to pull him out of the cage before the gnolls came."

Jorick brushed past Evin, leaned down, and grabbed Marten under his arms. With one big heft, Jorick yanked the older boy to his feet.

"Have you seen my father?" he asked. "Or your parents?"

Bet lifted her chin and regarded Marten over her nose. "Can you tell us where the gnolls were taking everyone?" she asked. "We think they're working for someone or something. Do you know who is behind all of this?"

Marten slowly shook his head, his eyes glassy. "I . . . ," he croaked, "I don't . . . We're all . . . doomed. . . ."

"Leave him alone!" Evin pushed his companions aside and put an arm around his brother's shoulder. "He's hurt, and he doesn't know anything, all right? Just leave him alone."

Jorick kicked one of the barrels. "Blast it!" His hand clenched the sword at his waist. "We were so close!"

"We can get close again without this boy's help, no need for histrionics." Bet held the *Practical Guide* open and looked at her map. Tracing with her finger, she said, "They took them into the slave mines. They could be leading them . . . hmm. . . ."

"What is it?" Evin asked, lessening his grip on the Marten and looking over Bet's shoulder.

"I heard the sounds of the gnolls earlier," she said to Evin, "coming from the hallway off of the room with the fireplace."

"I heard them too," Evin said. He looked at the map and found the room. The hallway led to a big, open room that the map called the "Goblins' Communal Area."

"The slave pens connect to the communal chamber," Bet went on, tracing with her finger. "And the halls are wider. I wonder, maybe the reason we haven't been seeing many gnolls is because they've all been convened in one place."

"You think they're gathered for some reason?" Evin asked.

"Maybe," Bet said. "Maybe whoever they're working for is there. And they wanted to see the villagers."

"Of course!" Jorick said, then kicked at another barrel. The wooden side cracked from the force of his boot. "It's always got to be something. So what do we do now?"

"We have to . . ." Marten wheezed. "We have to . . ." He trailed off, his hands twitching, his eyes scanning the ground.

Jorick stepped to Evin's side and lowered his voice. "Is Marten all right? He seems—"

"He's fine," Evin snapped. "He's just traumatized, all right? Let's go investigate the communal area. If the other villagers are there, maybe we can still save them."

"Follow me." Bet raced toward the doorway.

Evin put his arm around Marten's shoulders and side by side they shuffled behind her. He couldn't help but look at the side of Marten's head, worry sprouting inside him.

After twisting through the winding corridors and back through the fireplace room, they at last reached the open hallway that according to the *Practical Guide's* map led to the communal area.

The sounds Evin had been hearing ever since entering the passageway grew louder and louder. He could hear clearly now the high-pitched yips and yowls of doglike voices. These were more controlled than the laughing howls the gnolls had made before. It was almost as if the creatures were speaking in their own language.

Marten opened his mouth wide and began to wail, "Oh, gods have mercy on—"

Evin clamped his hand over Marten's mouth. His brother continued talking, his voice muffled by Evin's fingers. The younger boy had a lump in his throat, but he refused to let himself give in to fear and worry. All of the other villagers, all of the people he'd seen and remembered from his life in Hesiod, were counting on them.

"Keep . . . keep him quiet as best you can," Evin whispered. "I'm going to sneak ahead and make sure it's safe to keep moving."

Jorick nodded. His eyes darted over Marten, revealing an unease that matched Evin's. Jorick and Bet slid down the side of the wall, forcing Marten to sit down beside them. Certain that they were sufficiently hidden in the shadows, Evin crawled silently forward.

At the end of the hall, an old stone door lay ajar. Evin pushed through it and found himself on top of some long abandoned balcony overlooking a vast chamber. The chattering of the gnolls was deafening.

Still on his hands and knees, Evin picked through

the crumbling stone seats until he reached the edge of the balcony. He looked down through its rusted metal railings. Thirty feet down, the gnolls stood amassed. There looked to be hundreds of them, a sea of dirty fur, snarling snouts, jagged ears, and sharp teeth. The creatures stomped around restlessly, some even fighting at the edges of the room.

In the center of the room was a large bonfire. It looked like the creatures had felled several great trees and lit them ablaze. The flame was so massive that even from his position high up, Evin could feel the heat drying his cheeks. Smoke billowed from the giant blaze through a large hole in the stone ceiling, revealing the night sky.

Several of the gnolls rushed to a tall doorway and began howling. Taller gnolls dressed in heavy armor emerged from the entryway. The larger gnolls barked, bared their teeth, and brandished their weapons. The howling gnolls tucked their tails between their legs and went back to join the crowd encircling the bonfire.

The entryway cleared, and the larger gnolls gestured into the darkened hallway behind them. And then, the gnolls from the slave pens emerged, dragging the villagers behind them. They forced the chained villagers to line up against the outer wall. Evin couldn't make out anyone specific, but he knew his parents, his neighbors, and his friends must all be there. The gnolls shifted to look at the humans, salivating.

Evin swallowed and crawled backward as silently as he could until he reached the door. When he was safely out of sight, he stood and ran back to his friends.

"What did you see?" Bet asked.

"Are the villagers there?" Jorick asked at the same time.

Marten banged his head against the wall and muttered, "They are going to tear us apart!"

"Stop!" Evin hissed. He crouched at his brother's side and grabbed the boy's head in both hands. "Please, stop it."

Marten's pale, glassy eyes met Evin's. His lips opened and closed, opened and closed, but no more sound came out. Something was wrong with him, terribly wrong.

"There're gnolls, lots of them," Evin said. "And the villagers are there too. I'm afraid . . . I'm afraid the beasts might be planning to eat them."

Jorick leaped to his feet and pulled free his sword. "No!"

"Wait!" Bet placed a gentle hand on Jorick's shoulder. "We need to be quiet. We can't draw them to us."

Trembling, the boy sheathed his sword and nodded.

Evin let go of Marten's head slowly. He stood, not taking his eyes off his brother's face. "Marten?" he asked quietly. "We need to go now, quietly. Can you walk?"

"I can . . . ," Marten said. "I cannot . . . I don't want to die. . . ."

"Leave him," Bet said.

Evin spun on her, heat rushing to his cheeks. "I'm not going to leave my brother."

"He's acting unpredictable." She turned her back to Evin and started down the hall. "You can bring him if you like, but if he starts screaming and the gnolls come after us, it's on you."

Evin clenched his fists. He wanted to scream at Bet, but she was right. If Marten started wailing again, they'd all be caught.

"I'm going to go away for a few moments," Evin whispered to Marten. "But I'll be back, I promise. Can you stay here?"

Marten didn't look up at him. He just nodded.

Swallowing, Evin turned to Jorick and motioned forward with his head. Jorick nodded, and the two padded after Bet, meeting her at the partially open stone door. Together, all three crawled onto the balcony and peered over the edge.

The cavernous chamber was the same as Evin had left it: gnolls amassed around the flames, and villagers huddled against the outer wall. The gnolls were still salivating, still talking in their strange hound language, still moving about restlessly. But they hadn't begun to feast—yet.

"What are they waiting for?" Jorick muttered.

"I think they're talking in some other language," Evin whispered. He looked at Bet. "Maybe if there was some way we could understand them. . . ."

Bet nodded, then dug into her satchel. She produced her small spellbook and flipped through the pages. She held the book open to a page toward the end. "*Ahnqua,*" she said as she circled her wand around Evin's ear, then Jorick's. "*Fawel upwo.*"

As Bet finished her spell, Evin felt as if the world had gone silent. The sound of the gnolls' howling, the noise of the crackling bonfire, even his own breathing, all disappeared. And then, with a roaring *whoosh*, sound rushed at Evin all at once, the noises piercing his eardrums as though someone had shoved searing needles into his head.

Evin grabbed his ears, and at his side, Jorick did the same.

"What did you—" Evin began to say. The endless baying of the gnolls had suddenly ceased to be incomprehensible animal noise.

"We have been waiting too long!"

"We demand to know why the meat you had us steal is not fit for consumption!"

"These are not the humans we were promised!"

The noises the gnolls made were the same as before—all yips and howls and snarls—but somehow their foreign words were translated into fully formed phrases in Evin's mind. Even so, so many voices spoke at once as the crowd of gnolls grew more and more riled up that it was difficult to make sense of it.

"Who are they talking to?" Jorick asked.

Evin shook his head. He was about to respond when above their heads came the whooshing sounds of a giant pair of wings.

Evin craned his neck and watched as the answer to Jorick's question descended through the hole in the cavern's ceiling.

Chapter Seventeen

As the creature soared through the smoke and was illuminated by the raging bonfire, Evin realized he'd seen it before. Or, at least, a painting that looked very much like it.

"Bet," Evin whispered. "That's the monster on the *Practical Guide!*"

She raised an eyebrow, then pulled the book out of her satchel. Just as Evin remembered, a painting of a similar monster stared at them from the book's green leather cover.

Just like the illustration, the monster's body was an unusual mix of three separate creatures: in addition to a long scaly tail and dragonlike wings, its body and front legs were sleek and tawny furred, like a cat, and its hind legs white and hooved. Most unusual of all was the fact that the monster had three distinct heads. The one in the center was like a maneless lion. The head on the left was the horned and bearded face of a goat. The one on the right was the long-snouted, scaly head of a red dragon with serpentine eyes.

Quickly flipping through the book, Bet opened to the page with Zendric's notes on the creature. Beneath another painting of the creature—its dragon's snout opened wide to spew forth fire—the page was labeled "Chimera."

"A chimera?" Jorick asked. "Could this be the thing the gnolls allied themselves with?"

The creatures answered Jorick's question for him.

"You have kept us waiting for much too long!"

"We have followed your commands and we have nothing to show for it!"

The chimera circled the room, the great flapping of its wings dispersing the smoke. Evin's eyes watered and he muffled a cough as dirt flew into his mouth.

Finally, the chimera landed on a pile of stone on the opposite side of the room, where part of the chamber's wall had collapsed.

The gnolls' shouting grew louder and louder. They stomped their feet and raised axes and swords high. As one, the crowd surged forward toward the chimera, seemingly prepared to scale the rubble to attack the beast. The villagers cowered along the walls.

Rearing back on its hind legs, the chimera's goat head bleated as its lion head roared. The dragon head took in a breath, then opened its mouth wide. Flames arced from its jaws, exploding against the ground in front of the encroaching gnolls. Several of the gnolls flew backward, screaming. The dragon head roared.

Evin ducked and covered his head, his ears ringing. Bits of scorched stone fell from the ceiling and pelted his back like a heavy rain.

When the ringing in his ears faded, Evin realized that the gnolls had ceased their ranting. Peering again through the old metal railings on the balcony, he watched as the chimera set down on all fours, the eyes on all of its heads scanning the room. The gnolls stood back, silent.

After a long moment, the chimera's dragon head pulled back its lips and began to speak. In the sudden silence, the chimera's voice boomed through the vast room.

"I understand that you are uneasy," the chimera said. "And I understand that all of this waiting has been difficult. But you have proven loyal allies for now, and I assure you, once my plan sees fruition, you will have all the good meat you can handle, more meat than you could ever have dreamed of, so much that you shall never again hunger for flesh or thirst for blood!"

A murmur rumbled through the crowd.

The chimera flapped its great red wings and began to pace back and forth on its pile of rubble.

"We are all captives here," it went on. "Within these walls, magical creatures of all kind are kept caged as though we were mere animals. But soon, we shall rise up and free ourselves of our shackles. We shall burst through the wall that surrounds us and retake the lands that are rightfully ours!"

"The wall?" Jorick muttered next to Evin. Was the chimera talking about the great white wall that ran past their village and seemed to go on forever in either direction? Evin wondered. But the wall had always been there and always would be there. That's what Evin remembered. What could the chimera mean about bursting through it?

"Winged three head!" one of the gnolls called out from the middle of the crowd. "How can we know you are not lying to us? You told us that the village nearby was full of meat on which to feast! And yet, there were none! Only these."

Along the walls, the villagers whimpered. One woman fell to her knees as several of the gnolls turned to glare at the captives.

"A misunderstanding, I assure you all," the chimera boomed. "Our shared foes are trickier than I had anticipated. But know that it is now I who is three steps ahead."

"What is it talking about?" Evin whispered. "Do they not like human . . . er, meat?"

Bet shushed him.

"Bring these captives to my lair," the chimera went on. "I will need to make use of them for the next stage of my plan. And then, once everything is in place, the great wall shall crumble and we will be free!"

A great, howling cheer rose from the crowd. Lifting back its lion head, the chimera boomed out a growling roar that echoed through the chamber. Then, it flapped its two great wings and leaped into the air. It flew low above the crowd, so close that its claws almost grazed their heads. As the gnolls wagged their tails and jumped into the air, yipping their approval, the chimera zipped up and out through the hole in the ceiling, disappearing behind the billowing bonfire smoke and into the night.

With their apparent leader gone, the gnolls surged toward the villagers. The humans screamed and scrambled, trying to get away even though they were bound by chains. Evin's whole body went tense at the sight, terrified that the gnolls might start hurting the villagers, but the gnolls did not attack. They merely ushered their captives across the chamber and through the crowd to another hallway on the other side.

Evin, Jorick, and Bet silently crawled back from the edge of the balcony.

"We have to do something," Jorick growled.

"We will," Evin said, his voice sounding more confident than he felt. "They're not hurting them. They're going to take them to the chimera. If we follow . . ."

". . . Then we can save them," Bet finished.

As the three crawled toward the exit, Evin thought about the strange things the chimera had said about the wall and how they were trapped, and about how the villagers had been some kind of trick by some unknown foe.

What did it all mean? Why were the gnolls so angry about the villagers? And what about the wall? It was magic, yes, and it was definitely unusual. But he'd never felt trapped by it. Nor did he recall ever experiencing any monstrous, magical creatures until just the other day. If they were really trapped within some wall with all sorts of monsters, wouldn't there have been some sign of them years earlier?

But right then wasn't the time to think about it. Right then, they just needed to make their way out of the gnolls' underground lair and follow the creatures wherever they were taking the villagers.

He stepped toward the open stone door but stopped short, startled by the sound of thumping footsteps.

"Gnolls!" Jorick hissed, unsheathing his sword.

"Worse," Bet said. "It's Evin's brother!"

Before they could react, Marten burst onto the balcony, his eyes unfocused and wild. Tugging at his unkempt hair, he shoved past Evin and Jorick. Evin grabbed Marten's soot-stained sleeve in an attempt to stop him, but Marten's shirt ripped free and the boy ran to the edge of the balcony.

"Marten, no!" Evin hissed.

But Marten didn't listen. Seeing the villagers being forced along by the crowd of gnolls below, Marten screamed, "Evin, you have to help us! We're all going to die!"

In the cavernous chamber below, all of the gnolls ceased their yowling and turned as one to look up at Marten. Evin, Jorick, and Bet stood behind him, slack jawed.

And then, raising their weapons high and cackling madly, the gnolls surged at them, ready to tear them apart.

Chapter Eighteen

"What is wrong with you?" Jorick screamed, spit flying out of his mouth and splashing against Marten's face. "Why in the name of the gods would you do that?"

Marten didn't react. Instead, he brought his hands to his face and cowered, sobbing, "We're all going to die. . . ."

"We are now!" Jorick shouted.

"Stop it!" Evin yelled. "He doesn't know what he's doing. He got hurt and—"

"Now is not the time, boys," Bet said as she turned and ran around the stone door into the hallway. "Come on!"

Not wasting another moment, Evin grabbed his jibbering brother tightly by the wrist and raced after her. Jorick followed at their heels.

Staccato, laughing howls sounded behind them, and Evin looked over his shoulder just in time to see several of the gnolls climbing over the railing and onto the balcony. Madness flared in their eyes and drool dripped from their sharp teeth.

Evin shoved Marten into the hall and pulled Jorick through the doorway, then shut the stone door, knowing it would hardly keep the gnolls at bay for more than a second or two. Then, grabbing Marten by the arm, Evin raced forward. Ahead of him he could see Bet rushing down the dark hallway, her white robes billowing behind her.

They skidded into the room with the fireplace and the broken table to find Bet had stopped there to ruffle around inside her satchel. She pointed a finger at Evin, then at Jorick, and then at the table.

"You two," she said. "Shove that against the entryway!"

"Why?" Jorick asked.

"Just do it!" Evin and Bet said in unison.

Evin pushed Marten away from him and ran to the side of the broken table along with Jorick. They shoved and the table creaked across the floor. Bet produced a bottle of dark fluid from her satchel and began dousing the old wood.

"What is that?" Jorick grunted as he pushed. "Some sort of magic potion?"

"It's ale," Bet said. "I can cast a fire, but I'm not powerful enough to make it a huge blaze. This will help."

From the hallway, the howling laughter of the gnolls grew louder, as did their clacking footsteps.

"Shove!" Evin shouted. "Shove!"

Evin and Jorick leaped back just as Bet muttered a word of magic and pointed her wand from the fireplace to the table. Flaming logs in the fireplace floated into the air, hovered for a moment, then flew across the room. One flew so near Evin's face that he was certain it had singed his eyebrows.

The logs hit the table and the table burst into fire. Evin shielded his face and jumped back.

He could see the gnolls beyond the flames and through a crack in the doorway. They growled at the sight of the fire.

"Evin," Marten muttered, clutching himself around his middle and rocking back and forth. "We're going to die . . . we need . . . save them. . . ."

"Shh, shh," Evin said, grabbing his brother by the shoulders, attempting to make him stop rocking. "We need to run now, all right? We have to move."

Marten looked at Evin blankly. Evin wanted to cry, wanted to scream. This wasn't how it was supposed to be. His brother always knew what to do, was always level-headed. But the gnolls had hurt him, changed him, and now the world felt upside and out of sorts and—

"Come on, Evin!" Jorick shouted.

Evin turned to see Bet pull open the door to the left of the fireplace and run through, Jorick at her heels. Evin dragged Marten by the arm and followed as they blindly rushed down the dark hallways.

"Keep moving," Bet panted as they ran. "Other gnolls are going to take the path to that room through the mines and the slave pens. They'll be at our heels before we know it."

"Thanks for the reassurance!" Jorick replied.

They burst from the final hallway at top speed, splashing into the dark, dank water of the natural cave. Water soaked into Evin's boots and trousers, sloshing between his feet and the leather of his soles. He grasped wildly with his free hand for the cavern wall, pulling his struggling brother behind him.

Up ahead was the natural pillar that nearly cut off the passageway to the diamond-shaped chamber, the first room they'd entered in this lair. All four struggled to squeeze between the pillar and the craggy wall of the cavern. They emerged into the hallway and once again began racing.

"Get ready for the stairs," Evin shouted. "The trap fell, remember, so we'll have to jump up and—"

An axe flew out of the darkness and clanged against the stony ground.

Jorick shouted and jumped to the left, grabbing Bet and pulling her with him. Evin ducked to the right, dragging Marten down.

A gnoll stood behind them, cackling. It raised its blade at Evin and Marten, ready to bring it down again.

Jorick shouted a battle cry and lashed out with his sword, slicing the gnoll's leg. The creature screamed and stumbled, then rounded on its good leg to snarl at the boy.

"Go!" Jorick screamed as he readied his blade for the next blow. He met Evin's eyes, his jaw set in resolve. "Run, Evin. Save your brother. Bet and I can handle it!"

Evin didn't hesitate, couldn't hesitate. He hoped Jorick and Bet would be all right. Pulling the deadweight that was his brother, Evin burst into the torch-lit diamond chamber.

He skidded to a stop. Marten slammed into his side. Ahead of them, bounding down the steps that led to the surface were dozens upon dozens of gnolls.

Behind Evin, the sounds of Jorick's battle raged on. In the distance, he could hear more laughing howls echoing around the cavern.

Evin took in a breath, looked left, right. To his right was a doorway, the one in which the broken half of an axe had embedded itself. Evin dragged Marten toward the door, rounding past the fallen body of the gnoll Jorick had killed earlier. He flung open the door. A quick scan inside revealed a long, empty room.

A growling howl sounded from behind. As Evin pulled Marten through the door, a battle-axe whizzed through the doorway.

"Help!" Marten cried.

Evin threw his brother to the floor and slammed the door shut. The door latched, locking it.

The gnolls pounded on the wooden door, shaking it in its frame. Dust cascaded from the ceiling. Evin backed away. His legs ached. His heart thumped. Swallowing hard, he turned around. "Marten, we've—oh, by the gods!"

His hand flew up to cover his mouth.

Marten lay on the floor, staring blankly at Evin. His arm lay a few feet away.

Evin's mind went blank. Something was incredibly wrong with the picture before him. Marten, who had not stopped muttering and moaning since the moment he'd been freed from his cage, now sat in silence. And though his arm had been chopped off, there was no blood. There was no bone.

Through the hole in Marten's torso where his arm once connected to his shoulder, Evin could see hundreds and hundreds of tiny metal gears whirring and spinning, aglow with green magic. The same was true of the severed arm.

Marten wasn't Marten at all. The boy—the thing—he thought was his brother was some sort of magical machine.

"What in the—" Evin said.

At that moment, the wooden door burst inward, sending splinters flying. Evin stumbled backward and fell.

Dozens of cackling gnolls surged through the doorway, their weapons raised high.

Evin couldn't think.

He couldn't scream.

He couldn't fight back.

He couldn't run.

Nothing made sense: the chimera's unusual pronouncements; the boy who was a machine; his dream of a home on the other side of the wall; Bet's strange, one-sided conversation. Everything was off. Everything was confusing.

The gnolls loomed above him, ready to end his life, and at that moment, Evin was absolutely incapable of doing anything about it.

"*Eevik!*" a voice cried. "*Sueee cuedot!*"

Evin craned his neck and saw Bet standing right behind him. Gusts of air swirled around her, billowing her robes and her hair as she held her wand high and shouted. Her face seemed stern, older. An orange light sparked from the tip of her wand.

And then, in a shock wave, magic burst in all directions from Bet. It met the gnolls and they stopped, reared back their heads, and burst into millions of ashy particles.

The force of the magic hit Evin like a boulder, and he collapsed into darkness.

Chapter Nineteen

Evin dreamed he was back inside the large, decrepit house full of stinking, screaming children. He sat at the window and looked out onto a bustling city street. Next to him sat another boy. He was tall and lanky like Evin, and he also shared Evin's shaggy blond hair and pale blue eyes. Evin knew they were not related, but everyone called them brothers anyway because they looked so much alike.

The boy's name was Marten, and he taught Evin everything he would ever need to know about how to sneak into the inns, shops, and mansions of the prosperous city, to steal just enough to one day escape this horrible orphanage.

Evin stared through the window at the great white wall in the distance. It sloped upward as though curving into a dome. Attached to the northern side of the wall was a keep made of the same stone, a square tower rising into the sky.

Evin wanted to ask Marten about the wall and the house, about why he was here when he was quite certain that just a moment before he'd been a different person altogether, dragging a manic boy who looked like Marten except that he had gears instead of bones.

But when he turned to speak, a tall shadow stood in Marten's place. Inky robes flowed behind the figure, swirling like tendrils. Evin's chest tightened. Slowly, so slowly, the shadowy creature opened two yellow eyes to look directly into Evin's.

"What is real, Evin?" spoke a deep male voice.

The edges of Evin's dream turned as black as the shadowy man's robes. The screams of the rambunctious children and the sounds of their laughter and crying faded into an echo.

"Isn't this all a dream?" the shadowy man asked. "You are Evin of Hesiod, after all. And you have to save your people, your mother, your father. You must become a hero."

Evin struggled to speak, to tell the man that he didn't have a mother or a father. He was an orphan. But his voice felt trapped inside his chest. His lips parted, but nothing escaped except a gasp.

"Your best friend is Jorick of Hesiod," the man continued. "You have become an acquaintance of Betilivatis the elf wizard. You are on a journey through a world of danger and monsters, a world of adventure. Don't you want to continue your quest?"

The entirety of the world around Evin was now drenched in darkness, and though he struggled to recall where he'd just been, the memory was gone. All he could see were the floating yellow eyes of the man who Evin knew deep down was deadly.

Evin closed his eyes, and as he did he saw a vision of Marten. The older boy was crouched behind a bakery, pointing to a pie on a window ledge above him and mouthing something at Evin. The day was bright and cool. Birds chirped in the distance, but Evin could not hear what Marten was saying.

"Who are you?" Evin finally managed to spit out. "What have you—"

Evin's eyes shot open and he gasped for air. Harsh daylight burned his eyes. He shielded his face and sat up straight. His hand met cracked stone and tufts of grass. Heat from the midday sun sizzled over his skin, and he heard the distant sound of rushing water.

"You're awake!"

Jorick towered over him, blocking the sun. The shorter boy's somber face was smudged with dirt and dried blood.

Evin blinked, then looked around. He was outside, back in the ruins above the gnolls' lair. He recognized the fallen gazebo and the broken bell nearby, and to his right was the small river that cut the ruins in two.

The dream faded, disappearing deep into his brain. Evin struggled to recall what he'd dreamed about, but everything he'd seen grew hazy, indistinct. Try as he might, he also couldn't remember how he managed to get back up here. He remembered the chimera, the gnolls chasing them through the underground halls . . .

Evin looked up at Jorick. "What happened?"

"You don't remember?" Jorick sat down cross-legged next to Evin. "Bet did say you hit your head pretty hard. . . ."

"Bet?" Evin asked. "Where is she?"

Jorick shrugged. "Off in the ruins somewhere, preparing."

A flash of Bet casting a great spell appeared in Evin's brain.

He shook his head. "How did we escape?"

"Well," Jorick said, "Bet and I fought off the gnolls, then found a passage and dragged you through it. The next thing I knew we were up here and the gnolls stopped chasing us." Jorick shrugged again. "I'm not quite clear how we managed to escape, but I'm glad we did."

"Marten . . . " Evin muttered. There was something he was supposed to remember about Marten, something important . . .

A grinding of gears. A flash of green. The memories flitted through Evin's brain for just a moment.

"He's . . . " Jorick began, then swallowed. "He didn't make it, Evin. I'm . . . I'm really sorry. I tried to hold off the gnolls, but—"

"Oh good, you're awake."

Evin started, then twisted around to see Bet heading toward them. Despite their subterranean trek, she seemed none the worse for the wear. Unlike Jorick and Evin, her clothes weren't stained with mud or blood, and her long coppery hair seemed as pristine as ever.

Producing a strip of dried meat from her satchel, Bet smiled and sat down beside Evin. "Here, you should eat." She shoved the meat into his hands. "We've got a long day's walk ahead of us."

Evin took the meat, staring deep into Bet's eyes. Some memories churned within his mind. Flashes rose to the surface of his thoughts: his eyes opening after seeing Bet cast a spell that disintegrated dozens of gnolls; saying something, screaming something at her; Bet looming over him, lowering a wand that glowed with magic toward his head . . .

And though the memories were hazy at best, he knew they were real, and he was sure whatever they meant, it wasn't anything good.

"Evin?" Bet asked, tilting her head.

"I just told him about Marten." Jorick scrambled to stand beside Bet. He turned back to Evin. "Do you need some time alone? I mean, I don't really know what to do, but—"

Evin shook his head. "No," he said. "No, I'm . . . I'm fine. There's no time for mourning. We still need to find my parents and your father. What are we going to do now?"

"The villagers were taken away by the gnolls again," Bet said. "Remember, the chimera wanted them brought to it as its prisoners. We're going to follow their trail."

"And this time we're actually going to save them." Jorick offered his hand, and Evin got to his feet with a groan. His head felt woozy, and he struggled to stand.

Jorick cast a worried glance at Bet. "Do you think he's all right?" He helped Evin sit down. "Maybe you should rest here for a while longer. Bet and I will wait."

"All right," Evin said weakly. He felt too dizzy to argue.

Jorick and Bet huddled together and peered at *A Practical Guide to Monsters*. Evin could not take his eyes off of Bet. He knew something was wrong. He just couldn't quite remember what. He had this deep feeling that before he'd been knocked out, he'd seen something, remembered something that didn't fit with all that he'd experienced the past few days. All he knew for certain was that at this time the day before last, he was full of excitement at the prospect of a grand, heroic adventure, and that the night before, he'd felt a crushing sadness at the sight of the captured villagers and his brother.

Now, after the chase with the gnolls, something had shifted. He wasn't excited anymore, nor was he sad. He had brief flashes of memories that didn't seem to belong to him.

And he was certain that Bet knew something about it.

Chapter Twenty

After a few more minutes, Evin finally felt ready to stand and Bet cast her tracking spell. The glowing trail of blue sand meandered east, leading them toward grassy hill lands that Evin could see towering in the distance.

"It makes sense," Jorick said to Bet. "The *Practical Guide* did say that chimeras live in hilly regions, after all."

"Ah!" Bet replied. "Well aren't you just a little scholar?"

Jorick patted her on the back. "Not everyone can be as smart as I am, it's true."

They both laughed.

Evin wished he felt like laughing too. Perhaps if he could forget the nagging suspicions. Jorick slowed his pace to let Evin catch up with him. Bet parted her long hair behind her pointed ears and looked back at them, offering a smile before walking ahead. As she walked, the glowing blue sand rose up from the grassy plain and disappeared inside her satchel.

"You know," Jorick whispered to Evin as they hiked, "you were right. I just needed to give her a chance."

"Hmm?" Evin said, shaking off thoughts of dilapidated houses, glowing gears, and a shadow with yellow eyes.

"Bet," Jorick said. "She's not so bad after all. She's still sort of mysterious, but I did get her age out of her. Can you believe that she's turning seventy-four this spring?" Jorick threw his hands in the air and laughed. "Isn't that crazy? She's the best looking seventy-four-year-old I've ever seen, but I guess that's an elf thing. Don't they live for a long time and age slowly?"

Evin opened his mouth to respond, but Jorick continued to ramble.

"She sure is pretty, though," he went on. "In an elf sort of way, I mean. And she seems to like me too, though I'm not sure. She keeps making fun of me, but in a sort of friendly way, you know? Sort of how we do all the time?"

"Do we?" Evin stopped and met Jorick's eyes.

"What do you mean?" Jorick said. "Of course we do."

Evin looked at Bet, who was slowly hiking through the tall grass. The sun made her sleek copper hair glow like a mane of fire. Beyond Bet, across the empty, quiet plain, the hills loomed large.

"I just mean . . . ," Evin struggled to find the words. He turned to look back at Jorick. "I've been thinking about it, and I don't have any clear memories of us before the other day, the day the village burned. All I can remember is . . . this idea that we were good friends."

Jorick stepped back. "I'm sorry, you lost me," he said. "What do you mean you have an 'idea'?"

Evin bit his lip and looked to his left. He saw the great white wall in the distance. It had apparently curved somewhere near the ruins they'd left that day, for it was now heading to the north instead of the west.

Strange, dangerous ideas flitted through Evin's mind, ideas that, combined with his burgeoning memories and the chimera's words, made an unusual sort of sense.

"I mean," Evin whispered as he leaned in close to Jorick, "that I don't think everything is what it seems."

Jorick laughed. "Is this a joke?"

Evin looked into Jorick's eyes, his expression solemn. "You're not joking."

Evin shook his head. "I think something happened to me when I was attacked by the gnolls," he said, the words rushing out of his mouth quickly, as though if he didn't voice all of these ideas right away, they'd be lost to him forever. "Bet cast some huge spell and it killed dozens of those gnolls at once, even though she told us she was barely powerful enough to light a simple fire. And Marten, his arm was cut off. He didn't have blood inside, he had gears, and I think I said something to Bet and she cast a spell on me to make me forget. And then I had a dream about living somewhere else, somewhere without a family and where I didn't know you, and there was this man with yellow eyes—"

"Whoa!" Jorick held his hands up. "Evin, I know it must have been hard watching your brother . . . you know. But what you're saying doesn't make any sense."

"What are you two doing way back there?" Bet called back. She was standing beneath a cluster of wild apple trees. She held her hands on her hips and began to walk back to them.

"Listen!" Evin said, grabbing Jorick roughly by the shoulders and shaking him. "The other night, before we went underground, I saw Bet talking to herself in the ruins, like she was talking to someone else, but there was no one there. She was saying strange things that made it seem like she knew about the ormyrr before we ever saw it, and that she was guiding us somewhere. I think Bet is working for someone, maybe even the same foes that chimera was talking about and I think they did some magic on us and—"

"Shut up!" Jorick shouted. He raised his arms and shoved out of Evin's grasp. Snorting in anger, he backed away. "You're just saying that because you don't like Bet. I see how you two fight all the time. You're mad that someone other than you gets to shout orders for once."

"What?" Evin said. "No! That's not it at all! I mean, yes, she's bossy—"

"She's not the one who's bossy," Jorick muttered.

"But I know not everything is right with her. I just know it. And look at how you're acting now! Laughing and chatting with her like you're out on a casual stroll. Why aren't you worried about your dad anymore? Marten was your friend too. Why aren't you more upset about his death?" Evin shook his head, trying to sort it all out. "I think . . . I think her spell is wearing off. I think we're starting to remember what's real."

"You're crazy!" Jorick shouted. "I just know we're going to save my dad, and I . . . I don't remember really talking to your brother. I didn't know him well, that's all."

"But that's not what I remember!" Evin said desperately. "Or what my memories tell me, anyway. Tell me: Do you remember any time we spent together before two days ago? Anything specific?"

Jorick shrugged. "Yes. We were playing ambush in the woods."

"Before that!"

"We . . . we worked for our fathers and we . . . you wanted to run away. . . ." Jorick suddenly sounded unsure, his voice faltering as he struggled for memories.

"Three days ago!" Evin said, looming over his now confused friend. "What happened three days ago?"

Pacing in a circle, Jorick held his hands in fists at his side and muttered to himself. Evin looked desperately past him. Bet was coming closer.

"I woke up," Jorick said. "I . . . I ate breakfast and then went to my father's smithy and . . . and I—"

"See?" Evin said, lowering his voice. "Why is it so hard to remember? Why do we have to struggle to remember things that should be so clear? It's like sometimes memories just appear when we need them to, even though they weren't there before. Doesn't it feel like that?"

"It's just . . . ," Jorick began, then faltered.

"And think back to the slave pens," Evin whispered. "I didn't recognize anybody at first, but then memories of all of those people came back to me in a rush. Why wouldn't we think about or worry about people we supposedly have known all our lives? And the things the gnolls said about their meat not being good, and how the ormyrr said the gnolls had magical things with gears. I don't think those people were real—just like my brother wasn't real. They were magical machines!"

"I . . ." Jorick began.

"Did you two need a break?"

Evin jumped. Bet was there, finally having walked all the way back to them. She looked between the two boys, wide-eyed.

Evin knew he was scowling, but he couldn't keep himself from doing so.

"No," Jorick said. He offered Bet a smile. "Everything's fine! Now come on, we need to go save our families." Giving Evin a pointed look, he said, "I know my dad was taken by the gnolls to the chimera, and I will save him."

"That's the plan." Bet said. She touched Evin gently on the shoulder. "Is everything all right?"

Evin flinched and pulled back. Jorick wasn't convinced. Not even a little bit. Evin would need more proof than just his own scattered, confused memories. And until he had that, he couldn't confront Bet.

He shrugged. "I'm fine. Just still a little shaken up about what happened down below." He plastered on a fake smile. "We should hurry before we lose the sun."

Bet turned around to continue following her glowing blue trail through the yellow grasslands. Shaking his head at Evin, Jorick followed her quietly.

Evin watched them go. Now that he had voiced his thoughts, he knew everything he said had to be true. He had seen his fake brother's arm get cut off to reveal magical gears. Bet had cast some spell over him to make him forget.

And the vague memories that were surfacing now in his dreams—of a life outside the wall in an orphanage—seemed more real and true to him than any of the memories he'd had the past few days.

Jorick's memories were as messed up as Evin's were, he just knew it. Now, all he had to do was find a way to prove to his friend that their quest was a sham. And then maybe he could finally figure out what was really going on.

Chapter Twenty-One

"I'm going to make sure there are no gnolls around while you two set up camp. I'll be right back." Bet offered a wave and a smile before she disappeared behind a cluster of dark trees. Evin watched her go from beside their campfire.

They'd traveled through the day and had followed Bet's magic trail up into the hills. Night had fallen and they'd set up a temporary camp in a small clearing surrounded by towering dark trees at the base of the largest hill.

The two boys hadn't spoken for hours, not even as they gathered firewood and set up a ring of rocks to contain their campfire. But Bet and Jorick now seemed as close as two people could become in two days, laughing and joking and all together ignoring Evin.

Evin's suspicions had begun to waver as they'd traveled. He watched Jorick and Bet become friends, and he felt a little jealous and lonely. It made him wonder whether Jorick had been right: Was he just jealous of Bet's strength in dangerous situations? Was he just in shock because he'd hit his head and seen who he believed to be his brother die?

Then Bet disappeared into the woods. By herself. Again.

Evin's stomach growled. They'd eaten another bit of dried meat from Bet's satchel as well as some of the apples they'd pulled from the trees, but the meager meal hardly seemed enough, especially not with suspicion gnawing away inside of him as well.

Bet was probably off contacting her cohorts again, Evin figured. He imagined that's all she did any time she went off alone.

And that meant that maybe now Evin could get his proof and share this burden of doubt with Jorick.

The stocky boy paced next to the fire, sword unsheathed. Muttering to himself, he tightened his body into fighting forms and thrust his blade through the air.

"I'm sorry." Evin picked up a stick and poked at the fire. A log collapsed and sent up a shower of sparks into the night sky.

Jorick ignored him as he twisted his blade back and forth.

"I'm sorry," Evin said again, louder. "It's just I had all these memories and ideas all at once, and I felt so overwhelmed. . . ."

Jorick stopped and thrust his sword through his belt. Putting his hands on his hips, he faced Evin.

"So are you done trying to tell me we aren't really friends?" he asked.

Evin sighed. "Of course we're friends. Even if we've known each other for only a couple days, I still feel like I've known you longer. The truth doesn't change anything."

Jorick threw his hands in the air. "You're crazy!" he said. "Look, all I know is this: I grew up in Hesiod and everyone I knew from there was taken by monsters." Grabbing the hilt of his sword, he said, "My father made this sword. He taught me to fight. And I need to save him."

Looking up into Jorick's eyes, Evin he knew that no amount of talking would convince his friend of anything.

For a long moment, both boys were silent. Then, finally, Evin said, "Bet's been gone a long time."

Jorick sighed. "I told you, she's not so bad." "Then let's prove it," Evin said. "We are going to find her and see if she's actually looking for gnolls or if she's contacting her masters."

"I . . . no! Of course she's making sure no gnolls are around. What else would she be doing?"

Evin sighed. "Just come on. If she's looking for gnolls, I'll know you're right. If she isn't, then we can see what she's up to."

"I don't have to do everything you say, you know," Jorick said, his tone angry. "You're always telling me what to do and where to go and when to do things. I'm tired of it."

"That's only because you always ask me what to do," Evin said.

"So?" Jorick said. "I won't ask anymore, then. And I trust Bet, so I won't go with you."

Evin got to his feet and spread his arms wide. "Look, just do this one last thing for me, all right? If I'm wrong, then I'll never tell you what to do ever again. I just need to know if what I'm remembering is real or not. And I really want you to be there with me."

Jorick looked at his feet. "Fine. If it gets you to stop going on about all this craziness, let's go find her."

Evin grinned. It was the first time he'd done so in what felt like forever. "Finally," he said. "Now follow me carefully. Step exactly where I step. We need to be sneaky."

"I can be sneaky," Jorick said.

Evin looked Jorick up and down. "Just . . . follow me."

Leading the way, he ducked into the dark forest of trees. He carefully plotted a path between the trees and around bushes, avoiding any twigs or dry leaves that may crunch beneath their feet and give them away. The sky was clear and light from the almost full moon streamed through the canopy above, but still Evin moved slowly. All it took was one misstep to alert someone to their presence.

As they walked, Evin strained his ears. At first all he heard were typical night sounds—crickets creaking, night birds calling. But as they went deeper into the cluster of trees, he heard the sound of someone speaking.

Turning to Jorick, Evin held his finger to his lips, then gestured forward.

The two boys crouched behind a cluster of boulders. Beyond the boulders was a clearing, and in that clearing Bet sat cross-legged on the ground. Her white robes splayed around legs. A large book lay open in front of her. Though Bet was speaking, there was no one around.

"See?" Evin whispered. "She's talking to herself, just like I said."

Jorick snorted. "She's probably just casting a spell to track the gnolls like she did back in Curston," he said. "I can't believe I followed you out here. You've gone crazier than your brother." Brushing himself off, Jorick stood and started to walk back to the camp.

"No, I am not!" Bet's voice sounded icy with irritation.

Jorick stopped and slowly turned around.

"That doesn't sound like magic words, does it?" Evin asked, unable to keep the smugness from his tone.

Jorick sat beside Evin.

Bet fell silent. Her features twisted and her chest heaved as though she was struggling to control her breathing.

Then she said, "I told you, I am not interfering! What is the problem anyway? They're here inside the wall, they remain as clueless as ever, and they're fighting your little campaign, just like you wanted. Aren't you lot having fun?"

She let out a little sigh and rolled her eyes to look up at the starry sky.

"All right, fine," she said. "I . . . I guess tonight, then."

With that, she slammed the book shut. Muttering to herself and stomping heavily, she gathered the book and her satchel.

"That little witch!" Jorick hissed beside Evin.

"I told you," Evin said. "She's up to something."

Jorick reached for his sword. "I can't believe I trusted her," he whispered. He continued on, his voice rising higher and higher. "I can't believe I let her lie to me! I—"

Evin grabbed Jorick's shoulder and once again put his finger to his lips. Looking over the boulder, he expected to see Bet heading right at them. But she apparently hadn't heard Jorick's outburst. She disappeared into the trees in the direction of the unattended campfire.

Once she was out of earshot, Evin and Jorick stood still. Jorick's breathing was heavy, his fists clenched.

"She was lying!" Jorick said. "What was she talking about, that we're clueless, that we're fighting for someone? What is going on?"

Evin shook his head. "I'm not sure. But Bet was clearly made to join us for some reason."

Jorick began to clomp through the underbrush, back to the camp. "This doesn't mean I believe all your fake memory nonsense," he called back. "But I say we make her tell us what it is she's doing."

"Wait!" Evin darted in front of Jorick and held up his hands. "Just wait. You didn't see what she did to those gnolls. One spell and poof, they exploded into nothing. She's a lot more powerful than she's been letting on, and something tells me that our swords won't be any match against her."

"So what do we do, then?" Jorick asked. "Just let her lead us into some sort of trap?"

A smile slowly spread across Evin's face. "Actually," he said. "I think I know someone who also wants answers. Someone that could prove a big challenge for Bet."

"Who ?" Jorick asked.

Evin looked up the hill. Trees rose up its side, the bright moon peeking through their branches.

"The chimera."

Chapter Twenty-Two

"Where have you two been?"

Bet was sitting next to the fire as Evin and Jorick emerged from the woods behind her. She frowned up at them. The firelight cast shadows over her sharp, lovely features.

Evin shrugged as he sat beside her. The heat from the campfire warmed his face. "I've been thinking," he said. "Maybe we shouldn't wait till morning to find the chimera. We can't let our families and friends be kept captive by monsters any longer. They trusted me back in the slave pens, and we left them behind."

"That didn't answer my question," she said.

Evin looked into her eyes. Did she know they had been spying on her?

"We were trying to see if there's a good path up the hill," Jorick answered as he came to sit on Bet's other side. "One that would allow us to sneak up on the chimera without it seeing us."

The lie sounded so smooth that if Evin didn't know

better, he'd have believed it himself. He hadn't thought that Jorick had it in him.

Bet nodded and looked into the fire. The light reflected in her pupils. "Good idea," she said. "But what happens if we head up there only to find that army of gnolls waiting? And it wouldn't be safe to light our path, so what if we make noise and draw the chimera's attention?" She shook her head. "No, I think it'd be best for us to stay here tonight."

Evin remembered what she'd said in the woods to the unseen listener. Something about doing something with—or to—them tonight. Anger shot through him.

"No," he said, the word coming out more stern than he'd intended.

Bet glared at him.

He swallowed. "I mean, no, I don't think waiting is a good idea. But . . ." He paused, biting his lip. Then an idea came to him. "Actually, you may be right. We don't want to go stumbling into an army of monsters and their chimera general."

"We don't?" Jorick asked. He looked at Evin over Bet's shoulder, mouthing, "What are you doing?"

"Not all of us, anyway," Evin said. Standing up, he spread his arms wide. "That's why I'm going by myself."

"What?" Jorick asked.

Evin nodded. "I have a lot of practice sneaking through dark places," he said. "I'll scout ahead, just like I did back in the gnolls' lair. That way, if it isn't safe, we won't rush in tonight. And if I do make any noise . . . well, then at least only one of us will get hurt."

Jorick leaned back and nodded. "That sounds like a good plan."

Bet looked back and forth between the two boys. For a moment, Evin expected her to offer some protest, as so often she did.

Instead, she shrugged. "All right. Try not to die."

Evin let out a breath. Bet didn't seem the least bit suspicious. "I won't." Meeting her eyes, he smiled and said, "Be right back."

The moon had moved a quarter of the way through the sky when Evin finally emerged from the trees near the top of the hill. Beneath his feet, a trail of sand glowed faintly red. Bet assured him that this was a modification of her tracking spell that should make the trail only visible to only one person so as to not grab the chimera's attention. It should lead him directly to the chimera's lair.

As Evin peered from between branches, he saw that she was right. Where the red trail ended, the trees parted to reveal a clearing where the hill flattened out. At the back of this clearing, the hill continued its ascent into the sky, but there was a hole clawed into the hillside to create a burrow. Tree roots dangled from the burrow's earthen ceiling.

The grass in front of the burrow was sparse, most of it dug up by claws. What grass still remained was scorched black as though burned by flames. Or perhaps, the chimera's fire breath.

Most important of all, the moonlight revealed that all of the supposed villagers were here. Small cages were set all around the clearing. The villagers clustered inside of them in silence, their eyes glazed over.

The only thing missing was the chimera.

Evin crouched down and strained his eyes to look into the burrow. The inside was dark and he was unable to tell how deep it was, whether it was just a nook or the entrance to a larger tunnel.

Evin sat back and tried to think. If he snuck into the clearing, the villagers would see him, and like when they were in the gnolls' lair, they would probably start calling out. That'd be an unintentional alarm system that would send the chimera—and any gnoll allies that may still be in the area—running to attack.

Perhaps he could sneak around the clearing to the sloping hill above the burrow, then maybe dangle over the edge and—

The trees rustled above Evin's head.

Evin craned his neck back.

A flurry of claws, teeth, and wings descended from the canopy straight toward him.

Evin dived to his side just as the chimera's heavy body slammed to the ground. A great gust of wind rose up from the force of the monster's wings, sending leaves and dirt flying into Evin's eyes and mouth. He sputtered and rolled deeper into the trees.

Leaping up to his feet, Evin turned around. The chimera shoved itself between tree trunks, its wings flattened against its back. It opened up its lion jaws and roared, spittle flying from its teeth. Beside the lion head, the dragon head took in a deep breath. Evin could see a bright white light sparking deep within its throat.

"Wait!" Evin cried, holding up his hands.

The dragon head breathed out and a blast of fire shot from among its sharp teeth. Evin jumped headfirst to his left, landing in a ball. Beside him came the sound of a great explosion, and chunks of dirt and tree bark smoldered.

Evin tried to get to his feet to run, cursing himself for ever thinking this plan would work. He tripped over loose dirt and slid down the hill in a cascade of rocks and grass. He grabbed at a bush, but continued to slide down the hill, clutching a fistful of leaves. Again he reached out, this time grasping a sapling, and he hung on to stop his descent.

The chimera wound through the trees. With its wings held taut against its back, it seemed more lion than dragon now, and it bounded over the underbrush with ease.

"No!" Evin screamed, struggling to maintain his grip. "Wait!"

The chimera leaped and landed heavily in front of Evin and the sapling. Dragon and lion heads roaring, goat head bleating, the chimera slashed out with its claws. Evin ducked and the chimera's razor-sharp claws sliced through the sapling above his head. Half of the young tree collapsed to the ground and rolled down the hill.

The chimera raised its claws again, baring its lion's teeth while taking in another breath with its dragon head.

"Wait!" Evin screamed one last time. "I know what your plan is. I can help! Just please! Listen!"

Evin squeezed his eyes shut and gripped the lower half of the destroyed sapling with all his strength. Every muscle in his body shook. His brain screamed at him again and again for trying to do something so stupid as to sneak up on a deadly monster.

After a long moment, Evin realized that the chimera hadn't lashed out. He was still alive. But the chimera was still there. He could hear its snorting breaths, smell its sweaty fur.

Evin opened one eye, then the other. Moonlight reflected off the red scales of the chimera's dragon head, its wings, its long tail.

Slowly, the chimera's dragon lips parted.

"I'm listening."

Chapter Twenty-Three

"And you're sure it's safe?"

Evin looked back over his shoulder. Bet lifted up the edges of her robes with one hand so that she wouldn't trip over them. She held out her other hand to steady herself as they climbed up the last steep stretch to the chimera's nest and the circle of cages.

"It's perfectly safe," Evin said as he turned to look forward. He grabbed a branch ahead of him and made sure he had solid footing before hefting himself forward.

"I could have sworn I heard you screaming," Bet said.

"I already told you," Evin said without turning around, "that was one of the villagers. And the chimera was right there in its burrow, sleeping through it all, no gnolls in sight. Now is the perfect chance to sneak up on it."

Evin held his breath as he hiked between the dark trees. He expected for Bet to call his bluff at any moment, but Bet just climbed silently behind him.

"I think we're almost there," Jorick whispered from ahead of Evin.

The boy had leaped ahead partway up the hill, eager and anxious to find out what was going on.

Evin reached out and found himself grabbing at the same sapling that had stopped him from falling down the hill earlier in the night. The young tree had been sliced cleanly in half, Evin noticed as he hefted himself forward. The chimera's claws were ridiculously sharp, and he wondered again if he was doing the right thing.

She lied to us, Evin told himself. She stole my memories and she is making us go on some big monster hunt. Of course it's the right thing.

Shaking any remaining doubts out of his head, Evin quickened his pace and joined Jorick ahead. Behind him, he heard Bet curse quietly as she stumbled over the underbrush.

"Remember," Evin whispered to Jorick as they kneeled down in front of several bushes that lined the edge of the clearing, "keep as far away from Bet as possible once we get to the center of the clearing."

"Why won't you just tell me what the plan is?" Jorick whispered back.

"You'll see," Evin said. "Just keep away from her."

"What are you two whispering about?" Bet asked in a hushed voice as she came to crouch beside them.

Evin saw that for the first time her shiny hair was disheveled, her robes splattered with mud. Her eyes flashed with some emotion—confusion? fear?—and for the first time, Evin realized that everything that had happened since he'd met her must have been planned. Only now that they were going against orders did Bet seem even the tiniest bit normal. Or, well, as normal as an elf could be.

"I was just reminding him to keep quiet and follow me," Evin whispered. "And that the *Practical Guide* said we should spread out when facing a chimera."

Bet nodded. "All right."

"Let's go," Evin said.

Quietly, he pushed through the bushes. The branches rustled as they scraped against his clothes and skin. Then he was in the clearing, walking over packed dirt and brittle, scorched grass. Crouching low to the ground, he rushed as fast as he could across the clearing, to the left row of cages. Behind him, the bushes rustled twice more as the others followed.

Evin held his breath as he neared the cages, expecting the fake villagers to come alive at the sight of him. But they were as silent as the fake Marten had been after his arm was cut off. Their eyes were glassy. They didn't even appear to be breathing.

Evin looked to his right and saw Bet and Jorick similarly crouched as they headed across the clearing. Bet was in the center, fully exposed and clearly aware of it. Her eyes twitched as she looked toward the dark burrow. She clutched her satchel tightly against her side and held her wand high, prepared to cast a protective spell. Beyond her, Jorick had his sword unsheathed as he walked by the other row of cages. He peered into them, confusion on his face.

Holding his breath, Evin looked up into the sloping hill above the burrow. He couldn't see anything through the darkened trees.

Then, a shadow passed over the moon. In a flash, the chimera descended from the sky, its heads screeching and roaring and bleating.

Bet spun around and looked up. She didn't have even a moment to react before the chimera shot straight toward her. Wings unfurled, it slowed its flight. Its front paws slammed against her chest. The girl fell hard to the ground and dropped her wand. The creature landed, its front paws on her chest, its wings flapping slowly.

"Whoa!" Jorick shouted.

The look of fear on Bet's face was so real that Evin's insides twisted with guilt. But again he shook away those thoughts and rushed forward to stand ahead of the chimera, as did Jorick.

All three of the chimera's heads were tilted down to look at Bet's face. Parting the lizardish lips of its dragon head, it spat, "*Levethix. Pothoc vaecaesin levethix vi wuxu malsvir arcaniss.*"

Bet's breaths came out in short gasps. Her eyes were wide. Her hands clutched at the dirt beside her.

"Please," Evin said. "Sir . . . er . . . or ma'am. I don't understand what you're saying to her, and we need to know too."

The chimera's dragon head craned up, and now its dangerous eyes looked into Evin's own. "I am male," it said in its accented Common. "And I told this girl that she is a stupid elf wizard with evil magic."

"What . . ." Bet gasped. "What . . . is . . . going on?"

"That's what we want to know," Evin said to her, scowling. "We know you're working for someone and leading us into traps. Now tell us what you're doing or—"

The chimera's lion head roared. Its dragon head opened and spat out a small stream of flames that arced past Evin's head. It crashed against the dirt wall of the burrow behind him. Evin jumped back.

"Only I will ask questions, *munthrek*," the chimera hissed.

Evin backed away. "Yes, sir. Of course."

"Now," the chimera's dragon head said as it angled back down to look at Bet. "Tell me, *kosj vaecaesin* wizard: Where are your masters?"

Bet's body shook with terror, but she tightened her face and said, "I don't know what you're talking about."

"Yes you do," Evin said. The chimera's heads shot to look at him, and he held up as his hands. "Sorry, sir. Sorry to interrupt again. But . . . yes you do, Bet. I've been getting back memories, and I know that these villagers aren't real. Jorick and I were put in this wall for some reason, weren't we? Given false memories?"

Closing her eyes, Bet sighed. Her body began to cease trembling.

"I can't believe this," she said. "You have made an alliance with the very monster that stole your family from you, all because of some delusions brought on when you hit your head? This is all crazy. All of it."

"Not so," the chimera hissed. "Because I know that I have been trapped within this wall for centuries by your masters. These *munthreks* have now been imprisoned here as well, then tricked into believing the caged clockwork constructs are their families. We now share a common foe: you." The chimera opened his lion jaws wide and lowered his face so that his sharp teeth grazed the girl's chin and forehead. "Now tell me," he said with his dragon head, "where are your masters?"

"I don't know what you're talking about," Bet said

176

quietly. "I'm just a wizard's apprentice who made a trek to visit the Tower of Sorcery in Curston."

Evin paced back and forth. Beyond the chimera, he saw the quiet, soulless audience of the fake villagers watching.

"I know you're lying," Evin said. "And I can prove it. Chimera, sir? Could you tear apart one of the villagers?"

Jorick had stayed silent throughout the exchange, watching with wary eyes. But at Evin's words, his eyes filled with terror. "What? No! Wait, I—"

Evin reached out and grabbed his friend's shoulder, looking him deep in the eyes. "Do you trust me?"

"I don't know," he said, his eyes darting between the chimera and the eerily silent villagers. "We can't just . . . I don't . . . I don't know."

But Jorick's protests were too late. The chimera had already stepped off Bet's chest and prowled to the nearest cage. As it swiped at the cage's lock, Evin looked down to see Bet reaching for her wand.

Diving down, he snatched the wand from the muddy ground and held it behind his back. "Not so fast," he said.

Bet looked into his eyes, imploring. Strands of coppery hair were plastered to beads of sweat on her broad forehead. "You're making a mistake," she said.

Evin said nothing.

With a thud, the body of a female villager landed on the ground right next to where Bet lay. Scrambling, Bet pulled herself up to sit, and Evin saw that the woman was the gray-haired, kind-eyed figure of Mary Wright.

"No no no," Jorick muttered, looking on wide-eyed. "Oh no."

The chimera loomed above the body. Then, it swiped with its claws, tearing open the woman's chest.

Jorick flinched and looked away, but Evin could not tear away his gaze. Mary looked so real that for a moment he was afraid that he had made a mistake, that the memories he thought were real were the false ones after all, that he'd just ordered the death of an innocent woman.

But no blood seeped from the wide gashes on the woman's midsection. Underneath her flesh were hundreds of metal gears surrounded by a steel skeleton. Deep within the gears was a faint glow of green magic.

The mechanical woman slowly turned her head to look at Evin. A spark of recognition flashed in her glassy doll's eyes and she smiled. Parting her lips, she said, "Save us, Evin. We're all going to diiiiiiiiieeee. . . ." The word trailed off, her high voice deepening and slowing until she fell silent and her face grew slack. The green glow within her chest disappeared.

"By the gods," Jorick whispered. "You were right."

Still clutching Bet's wand, Evin looked up at Jorick. The shorter boy shook his head. One tentative hand reached up to touch his temples. "I'm remembering . . . this isn't . . . I don't live here. . . ."

"It's over," Evin said quietly to Bet. "Can you please just tell us the truth?"

Chapter Twenty-Four

"Y ou may begin," the chimera said.

They sat on the packed dirt floor of the chimera's burrow, around a glowing ball of magic that Bet had conjured. The light reached into the darkness, revealing that the burrow was a shallow cave after all, not a tunnel. At the back of the burrow lay a large pile of animal bones. Evin tried to ignore them.

The chimera sprawled against the wall, all eyes aimed at Bet. Though he'd returned Bet's wand, Evin had confiscated her satchel of magic supplies necessary to cast most of her spells—including the large book that apparently let her communicate with her masters.

Bet sighed and looked down. She fidgeted with her robes.

"I am very new to the order," she began, her voice hushed.

"The order?" Evin asked.

Bet nodded. "I'm not sure how large it is, but it is made up entirely of wizards. The order watches over the dome and the creatures trapped inside."

"The dome?" Jorick asked. "You mean the wall?"

"Yes. It appears to be a wall, but that is because the entire top of the dome is made up of transparent blocks so that the sky can be seen from inside while not letting any flying creatures—like the chimera—escape."

"What is the wall—the dome—for?" Evin asked. "Who built it?"

Still looking into her lap, Bet's face scrunched into confusion. "It's . . . I don't know," she said. Eyes wide, she looked between Evin and Jorick. "It's just always been here?"

She seemed unsure. Evin couldn't tell if it was an act or not.

Bet shrugged. "Working for the order, well, it's boring. It gets so tedious watching over the dome that from time to time the wizards . . . they play a little game." Swallowing, she met Evin's eyes. "They adopt two or three orphans from nearby cities, ones who have shown great potential for battle. Fledgling clerics and wizards and—"

"Rogues and fighters," Evin muttered. "Like us."

"Like us?" Jorick stared at Bet. "But I'm not an orphan. I have a father—"

"No." Bet couldn't bear to meet his eyes. "You just thought you did." She cleared her throat and went on. "You see after they have adopt the orphans, the wizards devise a campaign for them and place them inside the wall, near a fabricated town. The children are given new memories that are supposed to replace their old ones. Then they experience a catastrophe that sets them on a journey."

"Like a test?" Evin asked. "To see if we are fit for battle or something?"

Next to the boy, the chimera adjusted his position and lashed his tail against the wall. Evin swallowed. The creature was growing bored.

"Um, not exactly," Bet said, looking down once more into her lap. "The wizards take bets as to how long the children will last—or if they will even last at all. It is very rare for any of the orphans to survive, but there is always the chance. Those who bet on the success of the children pay the most gold pieces—and if they win, the order doubles the winners' treasure." She smiled faintly. "The order's motto is 'the greater the risk, the greater the reward.'"

Evin's whole body felt stiff, and his lip trembled. He stared at the side of Bet's face. She was still looking away from him.

"It's a game," Evin whispered. "It's all just a game to you. You and the other wizards just put us in here, took away our memories, and are planning to watch us die. All for your amusement."

"No!" Bet cried. "I mean yes, that was what they were doing, but you have to believe me when I say that I was against it. I am!"

"Liar!" Jorick screamed, jumping to his feet. "You were there, leading us along, making plans with your masters behind our backs. You made me think I had a father, a father who taught me every day how to fight and make weapons, who made a sword for me, who—"

Disgusted, Jorick turned away. He unsheathed his sword, looked at it in the glow from Bet's magical orb, then tossed it into the dirt. "This sword means nothing. It's just a prop."

"No, it's not like that," Bet said quietly. "I am the apprentice of one of the order's wizards, and they asked me to take part without fully explaining what was going on. They told me that you were willing participants, that you are orphans who hated your lives on the streets, and so you wanted to be here. It made sense to me. Memory altering spells work best when those whose memories are being altered don't resist."

"Well, I certainly didn't agree to do anything like this," Evin said.

Bet sighed. "I know that now, and since your memories came back, I suppose you must have resisted. I wasn't even supposed to be down here, just . . . Well, the last time they did a campaign, the chosen children weren't very bright and didn't know where to go or what to do. They spent days and days doing nothing at all, even after having found the *Practical Guide*."

"The guide?" Jorick asked. "Is that real or made up too? Is that Zendric guy your master? Is he behind this?"

"No," Bet said. "I mean, yes, the guide is real. Zendric was real, and he was really from Curston, before that city was razed when they built the dome. The book has been around for ages—all wizards have to study it before they are given their robes. The wizards figured that they'd at least give their chosen children a small fighting chance by providing them with a guide. The fact that I had to come with you in order to help you understand the guide, well, that was new this time."

"What happened to the kids?" Evin asked.

"Kids?" Bet asked.

"The last ones who were in here. The ones who weren't very bright."

"Oh," Bet said. "After watching them for a week struggling to find food and hiding out in a cave crying, the wizards coerced a band of goblins into attacking the children."

"Did the kids beat them?" Evin asked, even though he had a feeling that he already knew the answer.

"No," Bet said. "They didn't."

No one said anything for a moment. Evin let that sink in—he was right. They weren't expected to survive. The wizards wanted them dead. They'd taken him from within the stifling walls of an orphanage and trapped him inside another wall, all because they thought no one would miss him. He felt like he might be sick.

"Why you?" Jorick finally asked. "If you were new and didn't know much about this, why did they choose you to guide us?"

"Easy," Bet said. "Though I am many years old I look the same age as a fourteen-year-old human, and so they thought with me along, things might go smoother. First the gnolls would attack the village, then one of the wizards would pose as an old hermit and guide you to the *Practical Guide* and me, and then—"

"Wait," Jorick said, spinning around to face her. "You're telling me that they've been in control of everything we've seen? Including the gnoll attack? But I thought the chimera . . ." Eyes widening, Jorick rounded and looked at the chimera. "Are you working for the order, too?"

The chimera's lion head opened in a yawn and the goat head bleated. Resting its heads against its paws, its dragon head said, *"Pothoc munthrek.* Of course not. I'm a prisoner here too. I heard of the gnolls' orders to attack the village, and I interceded for my own ends. I convinced them to form an army under my command. After they had brought me the villagers, I planned to interrogate them and find where the wizards are hiding. Of course that was before I discovered the clockwork constructs have no minds of their own. I became aware of that wrinkle only recently. I work for no one, especially not those who hold me captive."

Bet cleared her throat. "I can safely say that no one ever told me there would be a chimera involved. I thought maybe it was just a late addition, and I did ask about it, but they wouldn't tell me much."

"So you didn't know at first what they had planned for us," Evin said. He pulled his knees to his chest and held them, looking past Jorick at the pile of bones in the shadows. "You must have figured it out after awhile."

"Maybe," Bet said. "But if it's any consolation, the order is now furious with me. I . . . I grew to like you two—"

"You didn't act like it," Evin muttered.

"Well, I did. They claimed I was helping you too much. Not letting you figure out how to get past the ormyrr was bad enough in their eyes, along with guiding you through the gnoll lair and breaking the lock on that cage. But they were especially mad that I saved Jorick from the trap and Evin from being torn apart by the gnolls." She looked into

Evin's eyes, her features grim. "I'm thinking that they're soon going to be taking wagers on whether I make it out of this alive too."

They grew silent.

"Last time I talked to them," Bet whispered after a moment, "I told them I think what they're doing is wrong. I was going to try and help you . . . in secret, and in my own way."

"Enough." The chimera's voice boomed, loosening dirt from the burrow's ceiling and sending it raining upon their heads.

"I grow bored of your explanations, *levethix*." As he spoke, the chimera stretched and rose to his feet. His hind hooves clomped heavily against the dirt as he began to pace back and forth in front of them. "If your words are true and you were an unwitting accomplice to the wizards who hold me captive within the walls, then you can help me escape."

"Help us," Jorick corrected under his breath.

"I don't know," Bet said, looking up at the fearsome creature. "The wizards on watch are very powerful, and their power will be even stronger when they discover they've been betrayed."

"She's lying," Evin said. "About being innocent in all this. Otherwise she'd help."

"I'm not lying!" Bet cried.

Evin jumped up, breathing heavily. "Prove it," he said. "Give me and Jorick our memories back. All of them. Take away the enchantment that's clouding our heads."

Bet swallowed and slowly stood. "I can't," she whispered. "Only the wizard who put the spell on you can take it away."

Evin took a step forward, coming so close to Bet that they stood nose to nose. She took a step back.

"Then you'd better take us to the wizard who did this."

Again Bet swallowed and looked down. Behind her, Jorick scowled.

A blast of flame seared through the burrow. "I said enough!" the chimera roared.

Evin, Jorick, and Bet backed away from the creature as he turned to face them, his wings spread wide. He seemed three times larger than he had been only moments ago.

"Enough of your explanations," his dragon head hissed. Narrowing his eyes, he looked among all three of them. "You three want to destroy the wizards, as do I. So let us take our fighting to them."

Chapter Twenty-Five

Evin had no idea how high up he was. He clutched the chimera's back with all his strength and buried his head into the fur at the nape of one of the creature's necks. He certainly could have opened his eyes and looked down, but then he knew he'd see the trees below looking like little more than twigs, and he'd know for sure that if he let his grasp loosen just a little he'd end up falling a long, long way.

Adventurer or not, Evin was pretty sure he was not a fan of flying.

His heart thudded in time with the great flapping of the chimera's wings. The wind brought up by the flight made his hair whip around his face and his clothes tug at his body.

Bet hung onto his waist, with Jorick behind her.

"This is amazing!" Jorick called out, his voice lost to the great wind.

"N-n-n-o it's not!" Up here the air was cold and Evin couldn't keep his teeth from chattering as he spoke.

"I agree with Jorick," Bet said. "This is—"

"No one was talking to you," Jorick interrupted. His voice was even colder than the air.

The chimera had wasted no time in taking off in the direction of the wizards' keep once the sun had risen. After Bet's confession, the chimera had cornered her and interrogated the elf girl in Draconic. She seemed to understand even though she responded to the creature in Common, giving directions to where the order of wizards watched over the lands surrounded by the wall.

As she explained it to Evin and Jorick later, the keep was a massive square tower that rose on either side of the wall. Magic kept it hidden until you were upon it, so only those who knew its exact location could ever find it.

While Bet had been talking with the chimera, Evin had found Jorick outside of the burrow sitting next to the body of the machine woman. The two boys had talked, vowing to keep watch over each other in the coming battle.

And now, here they were, miles above the earth and soaring north toward the great white wall that was, in fact, just the lower half of an endlessly large dome.

After many moments of silence, Bet whispered, "There it is."

Swallowing, Evin dared to open his eyes to look over the chimera's heads.

The wall loomed ahead of them, pearly white in the midmorning light. For a moment, it was all Evin could see—until the air in front of them rippled as though they were stones flung into a pond. Suddenly the view of the wall changed to show a massive structure attached to it—the keep, with half of the building on the inside of the wall and the other half looming outside.

The keep—the part of it that was inside of the dome—jutted forward from the wall, just as Bet had said. It was made of the same stone as the dome, its top covered with toothlike crenellations. Evin could barely make out shadowy figures peering between the crenellations atop the keep. One pair looked up at them from a large balcony in the middle of the keep that opened into a dark chamber.

"We are here," the chimera's dragon head roared above the sound of his flapping wings. "They appear to be prepared for us."

"What are you going to do?" Jorick called.

The chimera didn't respond. Instead, he stretched out his wings and dived to the top of the keep.

The wind tore at Evin, threatening to rip him from the chimera's back. He grabbed the chimera's flesh as tightly as he could. Though he desperately wanted to, somehow he couldn't make himself close his eyes.

Atop the keep, a half dozen men and women in various colored robes pointed at one another and the sky, screaming out things Evin couldn't hear. One wizard— a short man with a beard that curled down toward his feet—raised his wand at them. A fireball cracked out at them, but the chimera veered past it and the flames burst into empty air.

The chimera's goat head bleated a laugh. His dragon head said, "They think to try and use fire against me?"

Opening his dragon jaws wide, the chimera spat out a column of fire. It burst against the top of the keep just as the chimera reached it. Stone erupted into a cloud of white smoke, sending the short wizard flying into the air.

The chimera barreled through the billowing smoke, flapping his wings and dispersing the gritty cloud. His front paws and back hooves clomped across the top of the keep as he landed, attempting to slow his speed. The bump loosened Evin's grip and sent him bouncing.

"I command you to stoooAAAAAH!"

Evin saw the robed woman only for a moment before the chimera bounded into her, the goat head lowered. He butted her in the chest with his horns and sent her flying backward. She skidded on her back across the roof and lay still.

"Get off of me!" the chimera bellowed, shaking himself to loosen the grip of his passengers. "I will take care of these useless guardians. You three find the leader!"

Evin, Jorick, and Bet all slid from the chimera's back, and collapsed atop the keep. As soon as he was free of their heavy bodies, the chimera leaped into the air, his wings bringing up another cloud of dust as he spun. His lion head roared as his dragon head spewed forth a blast of fire. There were more screams as the flames exploded against stone and sent several more wizards flying.

"You heard him!" Jorick shouted as he got to his feet and unsheathed his sword. "Let's go!"

Evin dusted himself off and looked around the roof. There were now two gaping, jagged holes where the chimera's fire breath had struck, and several wizards lay unconscious. Across the roof, Evin could see several more wizards on the other side of the transparent wall that bisected the top of the keep, forming a barrier between the half of the keep that was inside the dome and the half that was on the outside. The wizards threw their hands in the air and opened their mouths as if they were shouting, but the thickness of the wall absorbed their screams. On the inner half of the keep's roof, the chimera busied himself by chasing a screaming man around the edge of the roof, lashing out with his claws and tail to try and knock him over.

In the northwestern corner of the roof, Evin saw the trapdoor.

"This way!" Evin raced toward the door. He looked over his shoulder and saw Jorick following him, his hand gripping Bet's arm tightly to drag her behind him.

"You don't have to be so rough," Bet complained.

"I don't want to hear it, you phony!" Jorick shouted at her.

Evin skidded to a stop and let a screaming wizard run in front of him, the chimera hovering at the magic-user's heels. Then, he dived to the edge of the wooden trapdoor, grabbed the iron handle set in its middle, and pulled the door open. A set of stairs spiraled down into the keep.

Another column of flame lit up the sky and exploded behind them as they descended into the depths of the keep.

The trio scrambled down into a long carpeted hallway one floor beneath the top of the keep. They veered past small wooden tables and plants in ornate pottery. Metal lanterns lit the way, and in between them, tall paintings depicting somber men and women in wizard robes lined the walls. Wooden doors were set in the walls at regular intervals, and at the end of the hall was another stairway leading down.

Evin could hear the sounds of more booming, roaring, and screaming above their heads as he led the way down the long corridor to the other set of stairs. He strained to hear whether anyone was on the other side of the doors as he passed, but if there were, they made no sound.

Finally they reached the end of the hall. Just as Evin began to lead the others down, two figures burst up from below.

The people—two men, one fat and balding, the other short and stick thin, both wearing bright blue robes and clutching long staffs—stopped. Both groups stared at each other.

"Betilivatis?" the skinny wizard asked.

"Colton." Bet nodded at the short wizard, then the fat one. "Klem."

The fat wizard—Klem—blinked rapidly, then asked, "What are you doing here with the game pieces?"

"Game pieces?" Jorick exclaimed. Letting go of Bet's arm, he unsheathed his sword and shoved past Evin. With a cry, he brought the flat edge of the blade down against the wizard's shiny head.

The wizard's eyes rolled back and he collapsed.

Colton raised his staff and began muttering a spell. The spidery words twisted from his lips so fast they seemed like one word. *"Ahnquaenteesev—"*

As magic began to glow around the staff, Evin reached out with both hands and grabbed the small man by the wrists. He tugged with all his strength and threw the man to the ground, where he landed with an "oof!" against the carpet.

Evin pulled Bet onto the stairs, then kneeled down. Before Colton could recover, Evin grabbed the edge of the carpet and folded it over him, then tightly rolled the man as if he were bundling a bedroll.

The wizard lay there, his face covered from the mouth down by carpet, his voice muffled as he kicked his legs uselessly.

"Sorry, Colton!" Bet called out as Jorick grabbed her by the arm.

They leaped down the steps two at a time, rounding down a spiral that seemed an even longer distance than the first set of stairs had taken them. Finally, they burst into a vast open chamber.

Jorick skidded to a stop and Evin barreled into his back. The chamber was some sort of great hall. Immediately in front of them was a long wooden table with high-backed plush chairs set across its northern side. The table was adorned with plates of roast bird, bowls of fruit, and goblets of wine, along with messes of parchment scribbled with all sorts of numbers.

Something hummed and glowed to Evin's right, in the northern half of the great room. There, the dome's clear wall bisected the room. A giant metal globe was embedded in the transparent bricks. Strips of metal with runic figures encircled the globe. Green magic shimmered through it. The strips of metal slowly moved, making the humming sound.

The chimera's roar echoed, and Evin looked to his left to discover that the chairs at the great table faced the wide balcony he'd seen from outside. Two tapestries hung on the walls on either side of the balcony. One was a sort of topographic map of a swath of land surrounded by a white circle. The other was a woven image that depicted two boys and a girl—Evin, Jorick, and Bet. Evin jumped back, and on the tapestry the image of a pale-haired boy that represented him did the same.

"I was wondering when you three would finally get here," a voice said from the balcony.

Evin's eyes shot away from the tapestry to see the backlit figures of two people standing on the balcony. They stepped forward into the light of the hall, and Evin took in a sharp breath.

One was the squat, hunched, white-haired figure of the Swamp Witch they'd met in the destroyed storehouse in Hesiod. Only now she wore respectable green wizard's robes. Beside her stood a tall man with slicked back black hair, a goatee, and severely angular eyebrows.

His black robes curled around him, tendril-like, and he peered at Evin with shrewd, sickly yellow eyes.

The wizard with the yellow eyes walked slowly down the steps of the balcony to the table. Hands behind his back and chin held high, he looked among Evin, Jorick, and Bet, a small smile on his lips.

"I have been waiting for you."

Chapter Twenty-Six

"Who is that?" Jorick hissed to Bet.

"It's my master, Sefron," Bet whispered back urgently. "He is the one currently in charge of the order."

Evin was barely listening. He knew those eyes. And the man's voice. They were from his dreams.

"Sefron is the one who took away our memories, isn't he?" Evin asked.

Bet nodded.

Sefron came close, his slender form towering above them. Evin heard the sound of the Jorick's sword unsheathing. He leaped in front of Evin, the tip of his sword aimed up at the man's chest.

"Give us back our memories and let us go home," Jorick demanded, "or I'll cut you in half!"

The edges of the man's lips curled into a smile and he walked directly to Jorick's sword. Jorick held the blade high, unwavering. Just as it appeared that the imposing wizard would impale himself on the sword, the blade curled down away from his chest as though the sword had become a limp noodle.

Jorick's eyes went wide. The wizard took another step forward. The sword wilted away. The man towered above Jorick, looking down his nose at the boy.

"Now why would you want to go home?" the man said, his tone condescending. "I worked so very hard to free you from a life as a street urchin, to give you a sense of purpose and a family. You were quite anxious to take up my offer when I presented it to you."

"That's not true." Jorick stood his ground. "I'd never agree to this."

Sefron tilted his head. "No?" His eyes flashed like gold and Jorick stiffened. His fingers went slack and the useless sword fell to the floor.

Holding his head, Jorick stepped back. "No," he muttered. "You didn't tell me everything. You said I'd be safe and you'd give me gold. You—" He fell silent.

Behind Sefron, the Swamp Witch cackled. She stood with her hands on her broad hips, her toady lips spread wide into a knowing smirk. "You three think you know everything," she croaked. "Oh, but you don't know a thing about—"

"Hush!" Sefron raised a hand in front of her face as though prepared to slap her. The Swamp Witch rolled her eyes and stepped back to lean against one of the high-backed chairs.

"And you." Sefron turned his yellow gaze to Evin. "You were quite ready to leave everything behind to go on a grand adventure. Didn't even hesitate. Said you couldn't wait to escape the orphanage's walls." The man's eyes flashed gold again, and a sharp pain lanced through Evin's mind.

A memory flashed in his brain: Sefron was in front of him at the orphanage, explaining what would happen to him within the wall. He saw himself, eyes wide with wonder, readily agreeing to join the so-called campaign at the risk of never seeing his home again. No questions asked.

Only, Evin knew that memory couldn't be true. Because though he was an orphan, Evin wasn't alone. Another memory bubbled up, that of his friend Marten. He'd never leave on some grand adventure without his true best friend by his side. Not unless he was forced to.

Evin steeled his features and looked into Sefron's yellow eyes. "You're lying," he said. "You're manipulating our memories again, delaying us until you can kill the chimera, erase our memories once more, and throw us back to fight more monsters for your amusement." Evin threw his hand in the direction of the table and its many parchments scribbled with numbers. "We won't let you go back to trapping kids like us inside this wall and taking bets on our lives."

The wizard raised his sharp eyebrows and looked at Bet. "I see you've been giving away some secrets," he said to her.

"Yes," she said back. "These campaigns are wrong. I told you that. I don't want anymore to do with any of this."

From the table, the Swamp Witch cackled once more. "Is that what you think this is about? Nothing is what it seems, little girl."

"Silence!" Sefron bellowed. He rounded on the Swamp Witch, his black robes swirling around him. Producing a spindly wand from the folds of his robe, he pointed it at the old woman. A great bolt of yellow light flashed and the Swamp Witch dived over the table, screeching.

"Darling, you know I love you," Sefron said as he lowered his wand. "But you really need to learn when to keep your mouth shut."

From underneath the table, the Swamp Witch laughed.

Evin narrowed his eyes and looked between the wizard and the woman beneath the table. Outside, he could still hear the commotion of wizards casting spells and the chimera roaring. Behind him, the giant mysterious orb hummed while Jorick still muttered to himself.

Sefron turned back to Evin, smirking. He looked between Evin and Bet. Evin didn't know what to say. He could sense that even Bet was confused. Maybe she was telling the truth after all.

And then, a great shadow darkened the room. Behind Sefron, the chimera whooshed through the balcony. He landed against the great table, sending plates of food splattering to the ground and papers fluttering into the air.

As he did, Klem and Colton stumbled out of the stairwell. "We're under attack!" Klem shouted. "One of the beasts found its way here and—by the gods!"

The wizard skidded to a stop behind Evin, Jorick, and Bet, keeping his eyes on the chimera. The great beast surveyed the scene with his eyes, panting for breath.

Sefron stood in front of Evin, watching him with those condescending yellow eyes. Beneath the table, the Swamp Witch giggled.

The chimera leaped from the table and bounded toward the humming metal ball embedded in the clear wall. Evin spun around. He grabbed Jorick by the shoulders and pulled him back just as the chimera slammed against the ball.

Green sparks exploded through the room. Bellowing, the chimera fell backward against the white stone floor. Beside him, the two wizards gasped.

"What is that thing?" Evin hissed at Bet.

"I . . . I don't know," she said. She held her head in her hands. "I know I did know, but now I can't remember, I . . ."

Flames arced across the room and lanced against the giant ball. As the blinding flash cleared from Evin's eyes, he saw that the ball was unharmed.

"The artifact!" the chimera screeched from across the room. "It is what is holding the wall in place! We must destroy it or we will be held trapped here by these wizards until our deaths!"

"No! You must stop!" Colton cried. The chimera roared and Colton raised his staff as though about to cast a spell. The creature prowled toward the short wizard. Yelping, Colton dived under the table.

That humming ball was all that held the wall together? Evin thought to himself. With this wall in place, with these wizards overseeing their real-life game board, more and more children would have their minds violated by magic, be forced to fight for their lives for the wizards' amusement.

Evin had spent his life trapped by walls: There was the orphanage, where he was always told he'd never amount to anything, that there was no escaping his life as a pauper. Then the inn in the false reality constructed for him by Sefron that Evin knew wasn't real, but still felt real. Now, the massive white wall kept him trapped in this land of monsters and magic, where he was expected to die for evil wizards' entertainment.

He was tired of it. Tired of being told what to do, of being trapped by those who thought they were better than him. He wanted to be in control of his life for once. Suddenly he knew what to do.

Before any of the wizards could react, Evin grabbed Jorick by the arm and dragged the boy behind him.

They reached the metal, rotating globe, but unlike the chimera, no magic cast them back. The wizards Colton and Klem merely watched in horror, did not even attempt to intervene as Evin grasped one of the strips of metal that circumvented the globe and pulled.

"Come on!" Evin shouted at Jorick. "You have to help me!" Evin's muscles threatened to burst from his skin, but with a screech of metal upon metal, he managed to loosen the piece and tug it from what was apparently a mechanical track.

Nothing seemed to happen—until Evin noticed that the runes on the strips of metal matched up with the surface of the globe. Straining his muscles even harder, Evin pulled his piece and matched the rune on its end with one on the globe—and the piece fell free of the globe, clattering to the floor easily.

Jorick pulled at another piece, and it swiveled easily in his strong grasp—but he couldn't get it free.

Jumping to Jorick's side, Evin shouted in his ear, "Push the pieces where I tell you to!"

Jorick nodded. Evin guided him to push piece after piece into position, matching up the runes and allowing more strips to fall free of the globe. As they did, the green light that glowed among the runes disappeared.

There was a great rumbling above Evin's head. Dust fell from the wall beside him as the giant transparent blocks began to shudder and slowly separate.

Chunks of magic metal fell to the ground at Evin's feet. The entire keep trembled. Evin's palms bled from hundreds of tiny cuts, his muscles burned, and his back ached. But he didn't care. All the confusion and betrayal and anger he'd felt the past few days gave him the strength to go on, to dismantle whatever this device was until finally, it was simply a heap of metal plates and crumbled gears surrounding him up to his knees.

As the last piece of the artifact fell, the trembling stopped.

Evin and Jorick panted. Everyone else looked on, silently. Colton emerged slowly from beneath the table and walked to Klem's side.

"What have you done?" Colton whispered.

Chapter Twenty-Seven

As sweat dripped into his eyes, Evin looked up and saw that the transparent stone blocks that had divided the room now hovered in the air like clouds in a spring sky. One floated near him, and he touched the glassy surface. The block drifted away as though as light as a feather.

"Bravo!" Sefron clapped slowly. "Well played, rogue." Sefron grinned at Evin then gestured to Jorick. "And you too, warrior. I overestimated your intelligence when I initially picked you. But I must say that you made a great team. Your respective tempers worked out nicely in helping me destroy the wall."

"You?" Klem bellowed, pointing a pudgy finger at Sefron. "What are you saying, Sefron? You planned this? But why?"

"We had a good thing here!" cried Colton.

Sefron turned to them and smiled. "Neither of you ever thought outside of the box, which, I suppose, worked out well for me. Now you have a choice: the two of you can flee and leave me to my plans, or"—Sefron aimed his spindly black wand at the floor, and a bolt of magic shot from its tip and sent white stone flying—"that could be you," Sefron finished. "Your decision?"

Colton looked to Klem, and Klem to Colton. Without a word, the two waved their staffs in the air—and disappeared.

"Now, to the issue of Betilivatis," Sefron said, turning to her. Bet began to tremble. She clutched her satchel close.

"Do not worry, my dear apprentice," Sefron said. He caressed her cheek, and she flinched. "I hold no ill will toward you. Without you, nothing would have gone as I had planned. And so, as a reward, I return to you your memories." His eyes flashed and Bet gasped for air. She clutched her temples as she fell to the floor.

"And you, boys!" he said, striding to Evin and Jorick. "You deserve a reward as well! For you see, no magical creature or man could have touched the artifact, and no normal human would ever be so dumb as to dismantle the one thing keeping legions of monsters out of the human kingdoms beyond the dome. However, you managed to do what I could not, and for that I am thankful."

Evin couldn't think in his exhaustion, couldn't understand what this man was saying. And then, Sefron was in front of them. The wizard's eyes flashed, and Evin's mind flooded with all of his true memories.

Only then did he realize what he'd done.

"No," Evin whispered. "No!"

Shoving past Sefron, he raced to the edge of the balcony and looked out across the monster-plagued lands that had been surrounded by the great white wall.

Everything made sense now. He could remember why the wall had been put there. Long ago, all the kingdoms in the area—including his kingdom, Dristoll—were under constant siege by monsters of all kinds. And so the people made a pact with an order of wizards—Sefron's order. The wizards would round up all of the monsters that plagued the countryside. Some people wanted the monsters exterminated, but the wizards refused. Their leader, a good wizard, would not allow it. Instead he vowed that his order of wizards would watch over the trapped monsters. To prevent any would-be villain from releasing the monsters, the order worked with gnome engineers to create a device that would lock up the magic keeping the wall standing. With the device in place, only someone of non-magical means could dismantle the wall—but no non-magical person could gain access to the keep without a wizard escort, and of course no wizard could teleport them in without being questioned by the many other wizards in the keep. It seemed like a foolproof plan.

Except Evin had just burst into the keep from the sky, on the back of a chimera who ambushed the wizards, keeping those at bay who might have been able to stop his actions. With his memories and mind clouded by Sefron's magic, he'd dismantled the device, thinking that he'd be saving future kids from death.

Evin looked back. Jorick still stood by the pile of dismantled metal, shell-shocked. The two of them had just broken apart the one thing keeping all of the murderous monsters from running free.

He'd just helped condemn who knew how many others to die.

To the left and right of the keep, Evin could see the remnants of the wall. Giant stone blocks now hovered, slowly rising into the sky and revealing giant gaps. A small band of gnolls tentatively approached the wall. They cackled then climbed past the blocks and raced to the lands beyond. Griffons and harpies soared above his head, diving through the gaps to freedom.

"I thank you, wizard," the chimera said from behind Evin. "Your plan was perfect. And now, I shall go." The creature roared. Evin turned to see the chimera racing at him, and he ducked just in time. The monster leaped off the edge of the balcony, unfurled his wings, and soared into the sky.

"What is this?" Bet screamed. "What is going on?"

Sefron lifted one hand to his chin and stroked his

black goatee. "My dear girl," he said, "you can't figure it out even with your full memories returned?"

Hands shaking, she looked up at him with eyes that shimmered with tears. "I trusted you," she said.

"Betilivatis," he said. "We wizards were trapped by this dome, just as the monsters within were trapped."

Bet looked at him, confused, and Sefron chuckled. "Oh, not literally, of course. I can come and go as I please, but doing so has only made me realize that no one out there cares about all we do to protect them. Long ago some insufferably good wizard decided that the wizards of our order should spend our days as guards, and for decades now our order has been stuck with the duty of watching over this dome. I created our little Monster Slayers game to help pass the time, but it's not enough anymore. Wizards of our caliber were not meant to waste our magic serving as watchdogs. No more!"

Looking down, Bet sobbed. "But all those wizards on top of the keep," she said. "You made me help you hurt everyone. Why?"

Sefron stood and put his hands behind his back. "Do not cry for those fools. They were content to sit back and play these little campaigns with the kingdoms' children, as though that were enough reward for the service we've given."

"So why didn't you just tear down the wall yourself? Why did you need us?"

"There was no way for me to dismantle the globe myself. When the wall was built, a committee of humans and wizards determined that the globe should be designed so that only someone with non-magical power could destroy it. That way the wizards guarding the dome could never be tempted to unleash the monsters without the permission of the kingdoms. But that wasn't going to stop someone like me. I devised a way to use the order's own game against them, to manipulate their human game pieces into coming into the keep and think destroying the wall was their best hope for escape. The chimera was noble ally in my plan. He wanted to destroy this keep as much as I did. But I knew he couldn't have done it alone." Sefron smiled down at Bet. "I needed someone to guide the game pieces through the campaign, someone young and lovely who they would inherently trust, like yourself."

Tears streamed down Bet's face. "I never would have done any of this," she said. "Never. . . ."

"I know," Sefron said. "And that is why it was necessary to play with your mind as I did with my chosen two humans. For that, I apologize."

"What now?" Evin said. Leaving the balcony, he climbed down the steps to stand in front of the table and its shattered plates of food and its scattered pages. He looked at Bet, at Sefron, at Jorick still standing silently by the pile of metal scrap.

"Are you just going to let the monsters run free?" he asked. "Are you just going to watch while they kill innocent people? Is your big evil plan to be the ruler of kingdoms destroyed by monsters? And why even keep us alive now that you're done with us?"

"Oh, I'll do more than watch," Sefron said, turning to face Evin and look at him with his deadly yellow gaze. "And who said that I am done with you?"

Cackling laughter rose from beneath the table, and Evin jumped back. The Swamp Witch emerged, her green robes stretched taut over her short, plump body, and she reached out at Evin with gnarled hands. Before he could react, her wrinkled lips whispered words of magic and he felt his body go stiff. He could not move.

Beyond the witch, Evin saw Sefron raise his long wand at Jorick and Bet. They, too, went still, though tears still made trails down Bet's cheeks.

"Gather them, sweetheart," Sefron said to the Swamp Witch as he lowered his hands behind his back. "It is still many hours before nightfall, and I have much more to do before I am prepared."

Chapter Twenty-Eight

In we go, that's a good lad."

The Swamp Witch pushed Evin from behind and he fell to the floor. Bet and Jorick were already inside. She had dragged their paralyzed bodies one by one up the stairs to the floor above, down the long hallway, and into this room. From where he lay on the floor, Evin could see a jagged hole in the white brick ceiling where the chimera had blasted it with his fire breath. Beyond the hole, someone moved, and there came the sound of metal scraping against metal.

"There we go."

Angling his eyes, Evin saw the Swamp Witch filling up the doorway, hands on her expansive hips. Catching him watching her, she smiled and patted her shock of white hair.

"You know, boy," she said as she came to his side, "I had a good bit of fun playing your guide at the beginning of the game. The Swamp Witch was my idea. I do so enjoy playing crazy. But I mustn't have you think I am a mere hag."

Producing a rope from within the folds of her robe, she set about binding Evin's hands behind his back. "My true name is Hennea Vudge, and I am Sefron's wife." She tugged the rope tight so tight that it bit into his wrists. Putting her lips close to Evin's ear, she hissed, "And I will have you know that I do not smell swampy."

That done, the Swamp Witch—Hennea—bound the wrists and feet of Jorick and the still crying Bet before taking their blades and Bet's wand and satchel. Hennea tossed all of the items in the corner, then retreated to the doorway.

"I will be back in a few hours. Feel free to talk amongst yourselves." With a wave of her hand, Evin felt the muscles in his legs and arms relax. Then, Hennea slammed the door shut.

For a long moment, no one said anything. Above their heads, the clanking of metal machinery continued.

Evin jerked his body until he managed to pull himself into a sitting position. He looked around the room. There was a large desk, some bookcases, and a chair. It looked to be some kind of study.

"So," Jorick said, his voice filling the heavy silence. "Who are you two?"

Bet sniffed and looked at Jorick. The question seemed strange after they had spent the past several days traveling together. But Evin knew what Jorick meant.

All the memories they had the past few days were in reality layer upon layer of magical lies put in place by Sefron. Lies that were meant to simulate the campaign so as to not arouse the suspicion of the other wizards in the order, but also lies that were meant to lead them to the keep, to destroy the wall, and to free the monsters just as Sefron had wanted.

Who they were the past few days was not, in fact, who they were for the many years before they'd come to find themselves embroiled in Sefron's scheme.

When no one spoke, Jorick cleared his throat. "We have some time to kill," he said. "So I guess I'll begin. My name is Jorick. I am from the city of Kellachstan, to the east by the ocean. Long ago, pirates killed my parents during a raid. I was left to fend for myself on the streets. I joined gangs of children and we fought in the sewers for some of the nobles. They came and placed bets on us, and we'd fistfight while they watched."

"Sort of like here in the wall," Evin whispered.

Jorick laughed, a sharp, barking sound. "Yes. Exactly like here, except back then I knew what I was doing, I wasn't going to die, and sometimes I got some coins or a hot meal out of it." He snorted a sigh and looked down. "But last week, my friend Geidan got me and him a job on a ship. We were going to be ship hands, do real work.

Then that wizard showed up and took me and—"

"Tied you to a table," Evin whispered, recalling the details himself. "Poured potions over you that burned. Read from his books. Pried into your head."

Jorick nodded. "Next thing I knew, I was in the woods looking for you. And I was a different person."

Beside them, Bet gulped down a sob. A shadow passed over the hole in the ceiling, and there came a clang. Evin looked up to see a metal grate with a hole in its center had been placed over the opening.

"You?" Jorick asked, ignoring the commotion above.

"My name is Evin," Evin said. "I am from the city of Dristoll."

All of his memories—his real memories—flooded him, and he spoke all he knew as Jorick and Bet listened on. He told them about how he'd lived for as long as he could remember in the Dristoll City Orphanage with dozens and dozens of other unwanted children, about how he'd always been alone until one day the owners brought in a boy off the streets who looked remarkably like Evin. He and the boy—Marten—had become good friends. Marten had learned from his uncle all the tricks of being a rogue before his uncle ran off and left him behind, and Marten in turn taught Evin everything he knew about stealth, about theft, about traps, about fighting.

"We were going to run away from there," Evin said to Jorick and Bet. "Marten and I had planned to sneak into the lords' keeps, steal some gold, and then we were going to go adventuring . . . until Sefron found me."

"I'm sorry," Bet whispered.

Evin and Jorick looked at her, surprised.

The elf girl looked up at them, her eyes red. "I know you must hate me."

Neither boy spoke. Evin wanted to blame her for all of this. But he'd seen for himself what had really happened when Sefron returned her memories. Her tears told him that this was no longer an act, that this was the true Betilivatis—not a scheming wizard, but someone who had been just as manipulated as they were.

"I don't hate you," Evin whispered, not taking his eyes off of her.

"I don't either," Jorick said. "So come on, tell us your story. Or was your whole weird, mysterious wizard act the true you after all?"

Bet's lips attempted to rise into a smile. "I am Betilivatis. I am from the elf city of Morronoir, in the forests to the far north. My parents did not accept my goal of being a wizard, and so I traveled to this kingdom and found a master in Sefron." She met their eyes. "I trained under him, and I knew he oversaw the wall, but I can promise you this:

218

I knew nothing of Sefron and Hennea's plans to dismantle the wall. No sane person would ever go along with that."

"No, definitely not," Evin said. "I don't think that either of those two seems particularly sane."

Above them came the sound of something grinding. Evin looked up to see sparks flying away from the grate. Beyond the windows behind the study's desk, the blue sky had begun to grow dark.

"What do you think they're doing up there?" Evin mused.

Bet shrugged.

Jorick looked between the two of them, face stern. "Do you two really want to sit here and wait to find out?"

"What are we supposed to do?" Bet asked, her voice forlorn. "We're bound in here, and Hennea is probably keeping guard."

Jorick rolled his eyes. "You can't seriously just sit back and expect to take this, can you? After what these two did to everyone? To us? We've got to stop them!"

Evin wanted to tell Jorick it was over. They'd done something awful, now they had to pay the price. But he said nothing.

Bet, however, smiled at Jorick. "Well, pray tell, what do you suggest we do?"

"Um," Jorick said. "Well, we need a plan. Evin?"

"Me?" Evin asked. "Why me? I don't know anything. I'm just an orphan, like you."

Jorick nodded. "Sure, but you were supposed to be the smart one! That's what my fake memories told me, and that's why I was always asking you what to do. Unless Sefron made those up too. I mean, you never seemed too bright to me."

Evin's despair drifted away, and for just a moment he felt a spark of himself again—the spark that told him he was tired of people underestimating him all his life. "Oh really?" Shoving his feet against the rug they sat upon, Evin turned himself in a circle. The rug beneath him caused friction beneath his trousers.

Then he saw the pile of weapons and Bet's satchel sitting by the door.

"Well, I suppose we could always grab our weapons from the pile where Hennea put them, slice through our bonds, arm ourselves, and make a grand escape," Evin said. Meeting Jorick's eyes, he said, "Looks like Hennea is the stupid one, not me."

"I knew those were there," Jorick said.

"Oh, wait," Bet said. "Before you—"

She didn't get a chance to speak before Jorick scooted across the floor to the weapon pile. Each thump of his body against the floor rattled the bookshelves lining the walls. A bird skull atop the desk clattered, its beak chattering.

Just as Jorick reached the pile, green sparks flew and Jorick fell backward.

"Ow!" He cried. "Why does that always happen to me?"

Bet shrugged. "I tried to warn you. Hennea likes to lay little magic traps to mess with people. Always makes Sefron laugh."

Evin furrowed his brow. "Are those two really married? She seems a bit, ah . . ."

"Old for him?" Bet finished, then shrugged again. "Like we established, they are insane. Seems like a perfect match."

Rolling back up into a sitting position, Jorick scowled. "I think I prefer life in Kellachstan," he grumbled. "Sure I had to box in sewers and eat out of the trash, but at least there weren't any magic or monsters."

"Hey now," Bet said. "I'm magic, and I'm not so bad, am I?"

"No," Jorick responded. "But you are slow to warn people who are heading into traps."

Ignoring them, Evin studied the room, looking for another means of escape. He noticed that the sky outside was now a deep violet, that the room filled with shadows.

A lamp appeared on the ceiling and grew brighter. Magic could certainly be handy, he thought to himself.

Evin's eyes came to settle on the desk—and on an inkwell with its quill. His mind raced until he remembered Marten's trick to untying tight knots using the strangest of objects. He smiled.

"Hey, can you two stop bickering and help me stand?" he said. "I have an idea."

Positioning themselves side by side, Bet and Jorick managed to give Evin enough leverage so that he could climb to his feet. As they watched, he hopped as carefully as he could to the desk. He landed hard against it, then twisted around so that he leaned back against the wooden edge. Feeling blindly with his bound hands, he found the quill and lifted it from the inkwell.

"Got it!" he said, and his friends smiled in encouragement.

Footsteps sounded outside, growing close to the door. A latch clicked as someone shoved a key into the lock.

Not wasting any time, Evin hopped forward and plopped down in a sitting position, his back toward the windows. Jorick and Bet hopped so that they sat in a circle.

The door to the room opened and the Swamp Witch waddled into the room. She rubbed her gnarled hands together as she looked over the trio.

"Still here," she croaked. "And still compliant, I see. How wonderful, as night is here and it's time for the real fun to begin."

Crouching down, she looked each of them in the eye, one by one.

"Now tell me," she said, "who wants to be the first to be sacrificed?"

Chapter Twenty-Nine

ennea the Swamp Witch cackled. "No volunteers?" she said. "Well, I suppose we could always draw straws. Now don't go anywhere, I'll be right back."

The squat woman disappeared into the hallway, the door slamming shut behind her.

"What?" Jorick cried as soon as the lock clicked.

"They are mad!" Bet exclaimed at the same time.

Evin gasped for breath. "She can't be serious," he said. "Can she? Why would they keep us alive if they were just going to kill us anyway?"

Pointing with his chin, Jorick gestured toward the grate above their heads. "For that, maybe?"

All three of them looked up at the grate. Through the slats they could see the night sky, stars faintly twinkling high above. But the metal of the grating wasn't a simple crosshatch—instead, the metal had been bent and twisted to form the outlines of runic shapes.

"Oh no," Bet gasped. Meeting their eyes, she slowly shook her head. "That is definitely a relic, not some covering.

The metal gratings form ancient words of power. They must be doing some sort of ritual!"

"What?" Jorick exclaimed. "How many evil schemes do these people have?"

The door burst open, and the Swamp Witch backed into the room, dragging something in with her.

"Just the one, lad," she croaked as she strained to pull whatever she was dragging through the door. "Everything else that has happened the past few days has all been leading up to this. Be a dear and get out of my way."

Jorick scooted back against a bookshelf as Hennea pulled a short metal slab into the center of the room. Upon reaching the space directly beneath the grating, she let the slab fall with a hollow thud against the round rug. Something rattled inside the slab, then quickly fell silent.

Looking between the slab and the grate, Hennea dragged the slab a bit deeper into the room. Satisfied, she stood back up, panting for breath. Placing her gnarled hands on her lower back, she leaned back, her wrinkled face contorted in pain.

"My dear husband will definitely need to find some younger lackeys after his ascension," she said.

Across the room, Jorick slowly began to scoot toward the open door. Evin held his breath as he watched. Maybe his friend could get out before Hennea noticed, find some weapons, free himself . . .

"Not so fast!" Hennea leaped over the small metal slab and slammed the door shut. She wagged her finger in his face. "Now is not the time to try and escape, not after you've been so good the past few hours, lad."

Face red and jaw clenched, Jorick looked up at her. "Go jump off the keep, you ugly old hag."

"Oh deary me," Hennea croaked, patting her wispy white hair. "I thought I already told you. I am not a hag. I am a wizard!" She pulled her wand from the folds of her robe and pointed it at Jorick. A bolt of green light shot from its tip, hitting him in the stomach. He doubled over.

"Jorick!" Bet cried.

"Betilivatis, hush up," the Swamp Witch said. "It has been quite a long day."

All three fell silent as Hennea went about examining the slab and making sure everything was in place. Only then did Evin notice its leather straps at the top and bottom edges.

Jorick's eyes darted between Evin's face and side, as though he was gesturing toward . . .

The quill.

Evin nodded subtly to show he understood. Making sure that Hennea's expansive back was to him, he mouthed,

"I'm working on it." He forced the quill's hard, pointed end into the tight knot that held his binds in place.

"My darling, are the preparations almost ready?" The deep voice of Sefron came through the slatted holes of the grate. "The moon is full and coming into the right position."

"Coming along, sweetheart," the Swamp Witch croaked as she hustled around the slab. "I will have one ready in but a moment, and then I shall give the word."

"Excellent."

Evin swallowed, twisting the quill and working it deeper into the knot. The shaft of the quill was softer than any other tool he'd used before and he felt it begin to snap from the stress. Holding his breath, he made one last twist.

"Hmm," Hennea said as she stood and tapped her finger against her sagging chin. "Eenie, meenie, miney . . . you." Lowering her finger, she pointed directly at Betilivatis.

"No!" Jorick cried.

"No!" Bet's scream echoed as the Swamp Witch kneeled over her and grabbed her by the middle. Bet struggled, worming her way out of Hennea's grasp, and the woman clucked in irritation.

"Dear!" she shouted. "Are you quite certain I can't use any paralyzing spells on these three?"

"If you do, I will have to kill you, my dear wife!" Sefron's voice called down from the roof of the keep. "Any spells cast on these children so soon before the ritual will taint their blood and thus taint my ritual."

"Blast," Hennea muttered, then shifted to get a better grip on Bet.

"Leave me alone!" Bet cried.

"Get off of her!" Jorick shouted. He struggled to get to his feet, his back still against the bookcase.

Hennea finally manage to pick up the girl in two meaty arms and slam her down against the metal slab with a heavy thud. Moving fast, she strapped Bet's arms above her head with the leather strap, then moved to her feet.

As she did, the knot keeping Evin's hands tied finally loosened, and his fingers untangled the rope around his wrist. Letting the rope fall to the carpet, he shot his arms forward and quickly worked to untie the rope around his ankles.

Bet struggled to breathe on the slab as Hennea pulled the strap around her legs, holding her in place. The woman dusted off her hands, surveying her work, her back to Evin.

"Perfect," she said, craning her neck to look up at the round grating above. "She is ready, my dear!"

"Then stand back," Sefron called down.

On his feet now, Jorick hopped forward, then stumbled over his feet and fell to the floor. "No!"

At the same time, the tip of a clear spear appeared in a hole in the center of the grating. In a flash, the spear sliced down through the room, directly at Bet's heart.

Her lips parted to let out a scream, though no sound escaped.

Hennea cackled as she watched the spear fall—and then let out a startled cry as Evin barreled into her back. The squat, round woman landed on top of Bet, her vast body completely covering Bet's torso.

Evin leaped back as the crystal spear impaled the Swamp Witch through her chest, killing her instantly.

For a moment, no one said a word. Evin trembled. His eyes shot to Bet's face, afraid that the force of the crystal spear might have sent it right through the old woman and into Bet's chest after all.

But Bet's eyes were clear, moving about in fright as she struggled to breathe.

Evin dived to Bet's side, unlatching first the leather strips that held her wrists and legs in place, then quickly untying the knots that bound her hands and feet. As he did, blood slowly began to seep from Hennea's body up into the crystal spear, as though her blood was being sucked up through a mosquito's proboscis. The spear itself rose up through the hole in the center of the grating, the weapon—or whatever it was—longer than the room was tall.

"Is everything—" Jorick started to say.

"Shh," Evin hissed as he struggled to lift Hennea's fat body up high enough so that Bet could climb free from beneath its weight. "Bet's alive, the Swamp Witch isn't."

"Oh, thank the gods," Jorick whispered. "Now can you two untie me?"

With a strained tug, Bet managed to free her leg from beneath the Swamp Witch's heavy body. The corpse thumped heavily against the metal slab, pulling the crystal spear down farther into the room.

"Is everything all right, my darling?" Sefron called down.

Evin stiffened, ceasing to untie the knot around Jorick's wrist as he realized that Sefron might find out what had happened, come racing down, cast his killing spells . . .

"Everything is perfection, sweetheart," Bet croaked without even looking up from the knots she struggled with at Jorick's feet. "Just switching to the second child."

"Ah," Sefron said. "Figures that little elf girl wouldn't have that much blood."

Jorick and Evin gave her a questioning look, and Bet shrugged. "I had many years to practice my Hennea

Vudge impression," she confessed as she freed the ropes from around the boy's feet. "It always made the scullery maids laugh."

"That was close," Jorick whispered when he was finally free.

"Very," Evin whispered. "Now we have to get out of here."

Bet nodded, then walked to the pile of weapons and her satchel. As she did, she waved her hand in the air and muttered words of magic. The spell around the weapons dissipated in a cascade of orange sparks.

Bet picked up her satchel, then rifled through it to produce *A Practical Guide to Monsters*. As Evin and Jorick gathered their weapons, she flipped through its pages before finding what she was looking for. Jorick smiled in relief to find that his previously noodlelike sword had hardened back into its usual form. Whatever spell Sefron had cast over it had faded away.

"Do you know what he's up to?" Evin asked.

Bet nodded grimly, then held up the book so that Evin could see. He could see a painting of a skeletal wizard in flowing robes, cradling an orb of blue magic on the aging parchment.

"I don't think Sefron's plan was just to unleash the monsters upon the kingdoms," Bet whispered as Evin and

Jorick studied the page. "I think he plans to wipe out all of the humans and lord over the kingdoms with its new inhabitants: the deadly creatures that are now freed."

Bet looked at them, her face pale. "I think he's going to become a lich."

Chapter Thirty

The hatch that led to the roof of the keep creaked as Evin opened it, and he ducked down, certain that Sefron had heard the noise and would come running. Behind him on the spiral staircase, Jorick and Bet stayed hushed, waiting.

Evin swallowed the lump in his throat and pushed the hatch all the way open. He peered up over the edge of the roof and took in the scene.

Ahead of him sat some strange contraption that Sefron had apparently been constructing, illuminated by the light of the full moon.

The crystal spear's long shaft, flooded with the bright red blood that had once belonged to Hennea, was connected to a glass tube that curved down toward a large, transparent alchemist's pot set in an iron frame above an open flame. The blood seeped into the pot and boiled before dripping out of a spout into a cauldron.

Sefron loomed over the cauldron, his yellow eyes not leaving its contents as he stroked his goatee. To the south, in the skies over the lands that were once surrounded by the dome, Evin could see the darkened form of winged beasts soaring to their freedom.

Looking down at his companions, he placed a finger over his lips and climbed silently onto the dark roof. He crept near the crenellated wall that surrounded the top of the keep as Jorick and Bet followed.

Sefron smiled, his eyes now on the crystal shaft jutting up through the grating.

"It's all done now, my sweet," Sefron called as he kneeled down and picked up a vial from his feet. Evin saw dozens more bottles of various sizes there, all empty. "You can come join me now."

He stood and uncapped the bottle. Taking in a deep, savoring breath, the evil wizard turned the bottle over and dumped its contents into the cauldron. As the dark liquid met the mixture, a poof of smoke rose into the air. Evin heard the distant sound of anguished screaming.

"Now," Bet hissed behind Evin. "We can't watch anymore. We have to move now!"

"Hennea?" Sefron called, spinning to face their direction.

There was no time to waste. If what the pages of *A Practical Guide to Monsters* said was true, and Evin had no doubt that it was, Sefron was about to transform himself into a powerful undead creature. And with all of Sefron's power, he would be nearly invincible.

Next to Evin, Jorick raised his sword high and shouted a war cry. He raced at Sefron, blade glinting in the moonlight.

Startled, Sefron didn't immediately react. Jorick barreled across the rooftop faster than Evin could have imagined, but just as the boy reached the wizard and brought down his blade, Sefron regained his senses.

"Eevik sueee eyeex!" he cried and he whipped his wand from his robes. A bolt of orange light exploded from the wand's spindly tip. Jorick ducked the blast and veered right. He skidded to a stop behind the wizard, then spun, brandishing his sword.

Sefron held his hands up high, looking back and forth between Evin and Bet to the west and Jorick to the east, all three slowly advancing on the wizard.

"And what is this?" the wizard said coolly. "You three have escaped? Then whose blood has—" The man took in a sharp breath, and for a moment his calm expression faltered before he once again regained his composure. "My Hennea."

"She's dead, old man," Jorick growled, not taking his eyes off of the wizard's outstretched hands. "We killed her, just like we're going to kill you."

Sefron sighed, then smiled a sickly smile. "I suppose it's for the best," he mused. "In my new state, I don't expect I'd have much use for a wife."

"We're not going to let you transform," Bet called out from beside Evin. They took another step forward, bracing themselves, waiting. Bet held her wand at the ready.

"Oh, I wouldn't expect any less of my little monster slayers than to try and fight me to the death," Sefron shouted back, then laughed. "But I suppose the question is now: Who is faster?"

In one smooth motion Sefron reached down and grabbed one of the empty vials, then dived toward the cauldron.

"Stop him!" Evin shouted.

Evin and Jorick raced toward the wizard as Bet began to wave her wand. Evin pumped his arms, daggers clutched in both fists, his eyes on the man who'd stolen his memories, manipulated him, murdered countless people, and had unleashed a monstrous horde upon the unsuspecting kingdoms outside of the dome.

Sefron leaned back from the cauldron, his vial full of a deep red potion, just as a flash of green exploded from behind Evin. A bolt of magic illuminated the sky as it flew from Bet's wand and crackled against the cauldron. The iron cauldron cracked and then crumbled, sending its gooey, crimson concoction flowing across the white stone of the keep.

At the same time, Evin and Jorick reached Sefron, their blades raised high.

With a flash of his yellow eyes, Sefron disappeared.

Both boys lowered their weapons just in time before they barreled into each another. They collapsed against the stone, their trousers soaking up the gelling potion.

"Where is he?" Bet cried as she raced to them, clutching her satchel to her side. "Where is—"

A shadow flitted behind her, and as Evin watched in horror, Sefron reappeared. Raising his wand—his other hand still clutching the vial of potion—he spoke words of magic.

"Watch out!" Evin and Jorick screamed in unison.

Bet ducked just in time, rolling across the dusty roof as a bolt of black magic flew harmlessly above her head. Sefron laughed.

"Too late!" he shouted, his voice wild, his hair falling over his crazed eyes. "You are too late!"

And then, he brought the vial to his lips, swallowing the entire contents in two big gulps.

Evin, Jorick, and Bet lay on the ground. They watched in stunned horror as Sefron tilted his head back and let his arms fall to his sides. The vial slipped from his fingers, shattering into thousands of glass shards against the roof. The evil wizard took one big, final gasp and then began to rise into the sky, hovering before the moon like the remnants of the dome that still floated there.

For a moment, the world seemed to stand still. Then, Sefron let his last breath out in a whoosh like a rush of wind. More and more air seeped from his lungs and swirled into the sky, flecked with bits of blood. As he breathed out, his cheeks began to sink, pulling tight against his skull. His fingers shriveled and his robes began to hang differently as every part of his body became skeletal.

His last breath ended with a swirl of magic worming from his open mouth, twirling at the air like some tendrilous tongue. His chest no longer rose and fell. His body was gaunt. His hair and his goatee were stark white.

Sefron lowered his gaze to look at them.

His tight lips pulled back much too far, revealing yellowing teeth. His eyes seemed strange, glistening as though gelatinous. Then, his eyes melted and poured down his decaying cheeks like vile tears. Deep within his empty eye sockets, pinpoints of red light glowed.

"From this moment forward, the world shall call me the Ebon Lord," he gasped, his voice like the rustle of dry leaves in fall. "I am the King of the Monsters. You shall all bow before me."

Chapter Thirty-One

"No," Bet gasped.

"Yes," Sefron—the Ebon Lord—wheezed, his voice like a rush of wind. "Now this world shall tremble. Now its kings and its queens shall learn why they should never cross one as powerful as I. Now they will watch as I tear their lands asunder and make them mine!"

As he spoke, he raised his skeletal fingers to the sky. His skin had grown translucent and the moonlight glistened off his stark white bones.

"What does the book say?" Jorick hissed. "How do we stop him?"

Fumbling with her satchel, Bet pulled free the *Practical Guide* and flipped through its pages, struggling to read it by moonlight.

Sefron the Ebon Lord cackled and Evin looked up just in time to see a ball of flame whooshing from his hand straight at them.

"Move!" He grabbed his friends by their arms and jumped to the side. The fireball exploded against the ground where they'd just been sitting, setting the sick potion ablaze. Beside it, the glass orb that had once contained the boiling blood began to melt from the intense heat.

"On your feet!" Evin cried. "Hurry!"

Jorick and Bet followed him, the elf not taking her eyes off of the book. They ran to the southern edge of the wall. Sefron did not follow, but merely hovered in the center of the roof, cackling madly. Two more fireballs flew from his fingertips, filling the night with an orange glow as they barely missed their targets.

"We have to distract him!" Bet cried. "Until we can figure out how to stop him!"

"On it," Jorick growled.

Before anyone could protest, Jorick grabbed his sword and ran straight at the hovering lich. Leaping over one of the holes blasted into the roof by the chimera, he skid to a stop right beneath Sefron and lashed out. The blade sliced through the monster's dangling robes and severed his foot.

Lowering his hands, Sefron looked down at Jorick. "Ouch," he wheezed. Then laughing once more, he lowered himself to stand right in front of the boy. As Jorick gasped for air and held his blade high, tendrils of magic reached out from the lich's ankle and grasped the severed foot. The tendrils pulled the foot back beneath the folds of the lich's robes.

"Did you find it?" Evin urged Bet. "Anything?"

Bet swallowed and pointed to a passage. " 'Attack methods,' " she read. " 'Various spells, paralyzing touch.' "

Gasping, she turned her attention to Jorick, who now backed away slowly as the lich advanced on him. "Jorick!" she screamed over the crackling of the fire. "Don't let him touch you!"

But she was too late. Scowling, Jorick had rushed the lich, bringing his blade down. As he did, the lich suddenly appeared to move three feet to his right in the blink of an eye. Jorick's sword sliced uselessly through the air as the lich floated behind him. Extending his slender, skeletal fingers, the lich touch the back of Jorick's neck.

Jorick gasped as his body went stiff. The lich pulled his hand back and tilted his head to watch as the boy collapsed to the ground, motionless but still breathing.

"Excellent!" Sefron wheezed into the night. "The new power within me . . . it is more than I could ever have hoped for!" Lowering his hand once more, tendrils of black magic began to swirl over his fingertips.

"No!" Bet tossed the open *Practical Guide* to Evin and faced the wizard, wand held high. *"Zeeast sueee usu!"*

Shards of ice crystallized in front of the wand's tip and sliced through the air. They burst through the lich's robes, soaring right through him before crashing against one of the floating remnants of the wall and exploding. Gasping, the lich turned his attention to Bet.

"My dear apprentice," he called out in his raspy voice as he began to float across the roof to her. "I had hoped to use your lovely elf blood for my ascension. But perhaps I shall stuff your head and keep it on my mantelpiece instead. It would be a beautiful conversation piece."

Wand clutched at her side, Bet strode forward. She looked down at Evin out of the corner of her eyes. "If this doesn't work," she whispered to him, "look for the phylactery."

"The what?" Evin asked.

Bet didn't answer. Instead she stood face to face with her former master. The lich hovered there, as though waiting in anticipation for what she might do.

"Sefron Vudge," Bet called out in a clear voice. "I command you to follow my orders."

The lich's body went stiff, and he lowered all the way to the roof, coming to rest on his feet. His skull-like face now expressionless, the creature walked toward her as though in a trance. Bet watched him, her chest rising and falling with her quick, frightened breaths.

The lich stood before her, silent. "Sefron Vudge," she said. "I command you to—"

Sefron's hand shot out, his long sleeve dangling from his skeletal wrist. He grabbed the girl by the throat, choking out her words and making her entire body go stiff.

"You stupid girl," he wheezed. "You think that I spent all these years planning to become a lich only to give out my true name to everyone I met?" He cackled, then released his grip, letting her fall to the floor.

Evin looked down at *A Practical Guide to Monsters*, desperately trying to see what Bet had meant for him to do. By the flickering flames of the fire that consumed Sefron's spilled potion, he read, " 'Best defense: Discover the lich's true name; destroy its phylactery.' "

That wasn't enough. Scanning the page, he found a note pasted onto it about the process of becoming a lich. " 'The phylactery may take the form of a box, an amulet, or a ring, depending on the wizard's style and personality,' " he read. " 'Most common: a sealed metal box containing magical phrases written on strips of parchment.' "

Looking up from the book, Evin saw in horror that the lich had raised its hand and was once more casting the spell of black, tendrily magic that he was certain would mean Bet's death.

A metal box. Evin strained his mind. The only metal, boxlike thing he'd seen anywhere near this ritual was. . .

"Bet! I've got it!" Evin leaped to his feet, pulled a dagger free from his belt, and flung it through the air.

Just as the lich began to finish his killing spell, the blade hit his thin wrist, snapping the bone in two and sending the hand flying into the darkness.

"You!" the lich bellowed, spinning to face Evin. "I suppose now it's your turn to feel my touch?"

Evin didn't respond. Instead, he ran around the perimeter of the keep toward the open hatch, pumping his arms and legs as fast as he could. The lich cried out phrases of magic as it tossed fireball after fireball at him.

Evin dived and landed hard against the stone steps, then leaped to his feet and ran down them three at a time. Above his head, the wooden hatch exploded into flames.

Into the tower Evin ran, bounding down sets of stairs until he reached the room in which they'd been held captive. In the center of the study, atop the rug, the slab still lay beneath the runic grate, Hennea's pale, drained body still impaled atop it.

Pulling free the short sword he'd carried all this time but had yet to use, Evin let out a cry and hit the crystal shaft with his blade. The crystal cracked, and Evin shoved at Hennea's body until the shaft broke and the fat woman rolled off the slab and fell into a heap onto the floor.

"You cannot escape me, human!" the lich's wheezing voice called as the creature hovered in the hallway. "You are nothing against me!"

Evin fell to his knees beside the slab, digging his fingers between its bottom and the rug. He strained his weak muscles. If Hennea Vudge could move this thing, then certainly he could. He had to.

"Nothing," the lich rasped, and Evin shot his head around to find the monster hovering in the doorway right behind him, watching him with his empty eyes, smiling his skeletal grin. His white hair and tattered robes swirling about him, Sefron the Ebon Lord raised his hand. Tendrils of black magic curled around his fingers.

"And now you die," Sefron said.

The tendrils congealed into a bolt of black magic and shot at Evin.

Evin heaved the metal slab up, angling it into the path of the lich's dark spell. The slab and the spell collided, exploding into a shower of silver sparks and strips of parchment that sizzled into nothingness as they fluttered about the room.

"Noooooo!" the lich wailed, raising his head to look into the sky.

As Evin watched, the lich's body trembled like a tree caught in a windstorm. The monstrous wizard's wail turned into a howl as his bones began to disintegrate into dust. Sefron's robes twisted and fell as his body dissipated, no longer held together by the magic of his phylactery.

And then, the lich's howls ended. All that was left of him was a pile of dusty robes.

The study was suddenly very, very quiet. Evin stood in place, almost paralyzed, as he looked down at where the evil creature had once stood.

Then he remembered that his friends were still on the roof, that the lich may have chosen to finish them off before making chase.

Not wasting a moment, Evin leaped over the lich's robes and raced down the hallway. He bounded up the steps, his body surging with adrenaline even though his aching muscles begged for him to slow down.

He burst onto the roof.

The potion that had been set ablaze was now almost burned out. The goo sizzled in black, tarlike bubbles. Sefron's crystal contraption lay in a heap, his many empty bottles shattered, the clear pot that had contained the boiling blood melted. The moon still shone bright overhead, and the great blocks of white stone that had once made up the dome's wall still hovered silently nearby.

Jorick and Bet stood together, hugging at the center of the roof.

"You're all right!" Evin cried. Unable to keep from smiling, he raced across the roof and leaped on them, grabbing them in his arms.

"You too!" Bet exclaimed, and all three hugged each other, laughing and rocking.

Jorick pulled back, putting Evin at arm's length. "What happened?" he asked. "We heard Sefron's scream, and then we weren't paralyzed any longer. How did you stop him?"

Patting Bet on the back, Evin said, "I found his phylactery. Like the book said, it was a metal box—the slab that Hennea was going to sacrifice us upon. He cast a spell and I threw the slab into it. Boom—no more phylactery, no more lich."

Bet laughed. "You really are a quick thinker, you know that?"

Evin grinned. "Thanks. But I learned all I need to know from—" He fell silent as the realization hit him. Evin ducked beneath one of the hovering blocks and walked to the northern edge of the keep, the side that had once been made inaccessible due to the wall. He placed his hands on one of the crenellations and looked north to the lands that had once been safe from monsters.

Jorick and Bet came to stand on either side of him, and all three studied the dark landscape. They could see more flying beasts soaring in the velvet sky in the distance, seeking out new homes. In the trees below them, torches blazed as other smaller monsters made their way north.

North, to where Evin could see distant towers rise and see the lights of kingdoms and cities. Cities like Dristoll, where his best friend, his mentor, Marten lived. Where countless other people, who were unaware of the threat coming at them from the south, lived.

"So what do we do now?" Jorick asked.

They fell silent again, contemplative.

"We could go home again," Bet whispered. "We have our memories back. Evin could go back and find his friend, go adventuring. Jorick, you could go and catch that ship. I could find a new wizard to study with."

Flames crackled across the sky ahead of them, briefly illuminating a three-headed, winged creature waging battle with some other flying beast.

"Or," Evin whispered back, "we could clean up the mess we helped make."

"What?" Jorick asked, looking up at him from the side. "You mean, keep slaying monsters?"

Evin shrugged. "Sure," he said. "We just met, but we seem to make a great team. At least Sefron was right about that one thing when he put us together: our strengths make up for our respective weaknesses. And hey, we have something most people don't: the *Practical Guide*, with all the details on how to handle anything we'd face out there."

Bet bit her lip and looked down. "My magic," she said. "Jorick's sword. Your stealth."

"You do like blowing stuff up, Bet," Evin pointed out. "And Jorick, you're amazing with that blade."

Jorick shrugged, his face solemn. Then, he patted Evin on the back. "So, 'old' friend," he said. "How about we go find our true friends and slay some monsters?"

About the Author

Lukas Ritter enjoys fancy coffee drinks, perpetually gray skies, bringing his own bag to supermarkets, and wearing wool socks with Birkenstocks. He currently resides in Seattle, WA.